SEPTIMIUS SEVERUS

SEPTIMIUS SEVERUS
Countdown to Death

by
YASMINE ZAHRAN

edited by
JONATHAN TUBB

STACEY INTERNATIONAL
LONDON

Septimius Severus
by Yasmine Zahran

published by
Stacey International
128 Kensington Church Street, London W8 4BH.
Fax: 00 44 0207 792 9288

Editor: Jonathan Tubb
Assistant Editor: Hugh Davis
Designer: Kitty Carruthers

British Library Cataloguing in Publication Data
A catalogue for this book is available from
the British Library

ISBN: 1 900988 194

Repro by: BBB Reprographics Ltd.
Printed and bound in Singapore by: Tien Wah Press Ltd.

Typeset in 11/13 Sabon Roman

Aknowledgements

For all their help and support in putting this memoir together, I would like to thank Jonathan Tubb, Tom Stacey, Max Scott, Emmanuel Barnard and Omar Masalha.

Contents

Foreword

by Jonathan Tubb

Often known as the 'African Emperor', Septimius Severus was born in Leptis Magna in Libya in AD 146. The descendant of a noble Tripolitanian family, his ancestors were, in reality, not African, but Phoenician, colonists more probably from the city-state of Tyre who had settled the North African coast in the 9th-8th centuries BC. It was the Phoenicians who had founded Carthage, and it is ironic that after the Punic wars which had brought utter destruction to that great city in the 2nd century BC, a Phoenician of the same lineage as Hannibal should become Emperor of Rome in that century.

It was perhaps his background, and the awareness of his background, which conditioned Septimius's life and reign. He chose as his second wife Julia Domna, the daughter of a priestly family from Emesa in the Roman province of Syria. In his policy, Septimius constantly looked east, as if to refocus the empire away from Rome in accordance with his own Levantine roots. Through his military campaigns, he annexed Mesopotamia and added extensively to the provinces of Arabia and Syria.

Septimius's non-Italian background brought a new perspective to the empire. His policy of equality for the provinces meant that 'barbarians' were no longer excluded, and although some historians such as Edward Gibbon saw this development as responsible for undermining the integrity of the existing social order, the empire undoubtedly took on a more humane aspect, with realistic laws and a genuine concern for the oppressed.

The events and details of Septimius Severus's reign are to be found in several excellent biographies. This well-researched study is different, however, in that its author, Yasmine Zahran, by casting the historical narrative in the form of a first-person memoir, has managed to examine the man behind the events, and to explore to the full the oriental side of this complex personality. The result is fascinating.

JNT
February 2000

FIRST NIGHT

The Dream

Eboracum (York)
29 January AD *211*

I, Imperator, Caesar, Lucius, Septimius, Severus Pius, Pertinax, Augustus, Pontifex Maximus, Arabicus, Adiabenicus, Parthicus Maximus, Imperator XI, Consul III, Proconsul, Father of the Country, Holder of the Tribunician Authority XVIII, Defender of the World, Britannicus Maximus, son of the divine Marcus Antoninus Pius, Germanicus, Sarmaticus, brother of the divine Commodus, grandson of the divine Hadrian, lineal descendant of the divine Trajan and the divine Nerva, I, who they call invincible[1] and most fortunate of men am nothing but an old cripple, ravaged by disease, lying on a narrow deathbed in a barbarous land of darkness. I knew from the start that my hour had come. Last night I had a dream confirming what the stars had foretold before I left Rome. It is given to few men to know the hour of their death, knowledge which some would attribute to the grace of the gods' others to their malediction and displeasure; for what mortal can await with composure the known hour of his extinction?

I shall dictate this intimate memoir in Greek. I would have preferred to write it myself but my hand is withered and can no more hold the pen, although I have the consolation that the chief of the Greek Secretariat will correct my grammar if not my style, for at this precise moment when the words are rushing from my feverish brain, I cannot take time to ponder over the elegance of composition or the turning of a phrase.

Yes, the gods have forced me to speak, to reveal the obverse of the coin of the multiple man called Severus and show to the light the face which neither his family nor his companions, nor the senate, the army nor the public have ever seen.

This countdown to death will only cease on my last breath. To those of my generation who read the autobiography[2] I wrote seventeen years ago and who must have been bored to death with its banalities, I give assurance that this memoir will amuse you; it might even provoke you to reflect on human frailty, for all our deeds are subject to a thousand chances and the greater a man's success the greater his misfortune. To the youths born during my reign, I hope it will expand your awareness of the glory of this universal empire, built with the blood of your elders, which embraces the inhabited world and all the human race. It is you who, when your turn comes, will be called upon to carry the burden.

I am, alas, unable to begin this memoir as did my adopted father, Marcus Aurelius, who started his meditations by enumerating all those from whom he learned, including all his family, tutors, friends and philosophers.[3] It is possible that, unlike my father, I only learned when it was too late. I learned sometimes from events, on occasion from observing the cycles of nature, sometimes from the stars and often from remarkable men who crossed my path. In one way or another this memoir is a record, even a history, but above all it is a remedy. Livy wrote in his *War with Hannibal*, in one of my favourite passages, 'The study of history is the best medicine for a sick mind, for in history you have a record of the infinite variety of human experience - and in that record you can find yourself, and your country, both examples and warnings.'[4] This, then, is my history and also that of Rome. My destiny has been linked with hers, and in delving into our past, mine and hers, I hope to find, like Livy, the best medicine for the aches of the body and the agony of the mind.

I have reserved the seven nights left to me solely for dictation, and I have instructed my chamberlain that under no pretext should I be disturbed. The days, however, will be spent in preparation for the spring campaign, now that winter is almost over. I shall deal also with the routine administration of the empire, pretending that I shall soon be back in Rome; the Adventus Augusti denarius I have issued has reassured the Romans by announcing my immediate return. It is a strange quirk of fate that I shall die in Britain, a land of cold and darkness, of thick mists arising from the marshes with a perpetual atmosphere of gloom[5], instead of dying on the desert's edge with war cries ringing in my ears and the sun reflected on my shield. Why have the stars decreed that I die amongst fierce tattooed savages, naked and painted blue?[6]

Fog and mist penetrate my chamber and icy winds my joints. I crave the sun; I am a devotee of the sun. I can never be warm in this damp palace[7], in this hole in the ground they call Eboracum, capital of Lower Britain, headquarters of the northern command and temporary capital of the Roman Empire.

Messengers and emissaries come daily by land and sea with deputations from the citizens of Rome and petitions and lawsuits from the furthest corners of the empire. Only this morning I received some sleek polished Greeks, ambassadors from Ephesus, who fatigued me with their disputes and flattery, yet amused me with their sharp wits.[8]

I am weary. I cannot tolerate the atrocious pain that invades every muscle and from which these stupid doctors bring no relief. I refuse to see them, although they are keeping vigil in the palace. The fools are trying to justify the fees they receive from the Imperial Treasury. Their herbs and concoctions made from animal intestines and fish livers make me worse. I ordered them not to give me medicine made from snake poison, but who knows? I do not trust them. I shudder when their fat greasy hands touch my withered body as if it were a discarded object, and I refuse to answer their idiotic questions. 'Caesar, did your bowels move today?' If only Galen was alive to give me the medicine he prescribed to my father Marcus Aurelius. But the doctors' calls are not the only ones I dread: I cannot bear the visits of the Caledonian chiefs who come daily to hear news of my illness, perhaps of my death, calculating in their barbarian minds how they will stab my legions in the back when I am gone and make a treaty with my deviant son. As Emperor of Rome, I cannot refuse to see newly conquered subjects as I do the doctors. The windows have to be opened when they leave and two incense burners are hardly enough to cover their unwashed smells. They stamp their feet awkwardly and swing their giant bodies and shake their blond locks caked with dirt. They have not yet learned how to behave in the presence of a Roman Emperor.

After they leave I ask myself why I am fighting in Britain. There are two answers to this question: The world knows only one; the other, the secret answer, known only to myself, is to be found in the Egyptian sacred book which foretells the rise and fall of individuals, nations, kingdoms and empires. The book of prophecy and divination indicates clearly two rising areas within what I believe to be the present boundaries of the Roman Empire. Their rise coincides in time with our present cycle, but this cycle lasts more than two thousand years during which empires will rise and fall. The translated Greek text of the sacred book speaks of their emergence from barbarism to the forefront of world affairs and I, in my vanity, attribute their advance to the civilising influence of Rome and wish to be an agent in this process. As if the cycles of fate which govern our destiny would pay heed to a mere Roman Emperor!

One area corresponds to a distant island in the west which I take to be Britain, the other to a vast desert wasteland in the east, which I believe to be Arabia. One of the areas will form an empire that will rule the land and the seas, the other will burst out of its boundaries with tremendous energy and conquer a great part of the civilized world; its influence will outlive its conquests. According to my calculations and from indications in the text one of these events will occur in about four centuries from now, the other will be in about fifteen centuries; but I do not know which will emerge first, the area in the east or that in the west, and in my passion, haste and blind ignorance, I gambled on the island in the west. This arrogance must have displeased the gods, for wasn't I meddling with matters beyond human control? My father, Marcus Aurelius, used to say, 'All things from eternity are of like forms and come around in a circle, and these circles are ordained and reshaped by the gods.'[9] I passed the measure and the balance that should be observed in all things. I did not stay in the place allotted to me by destiny. I, a mortal, who for a minute in Egypt believed he was divine, encroached upon the gods, and I have received my punishment for trying to interfere with the natural order of things. I committed the greatest sin a man could commit in the eyes of the gods: I believed in my own power and Nemesis, the goddess of vengeance, punished my pride and my presumption. My punishment and my torture lie in the incessant suspicion that I chose the wrong nerea, the further from our time, and this was due to my misinterpretation of the book of prophecy. Although mainly translated into Greek, the symbols and a great part of the text are still in hieroglyphics which remain unintelligible to me.

My suspicion became more of a certainty when I saw the state of the British barbarians, for it will take more than a few centuries to make of them a civilised and imperial nation. Papinian, my friend and praetorian prefect, is always teasing me about civilising the British. He does not know the reason for my efforts. But then I find it hard to see the primitive bedouin tribes of Arabia as conquerors either, although I spared no effort and expense fortifying the provinces of Syria and Arabia against their incursions. Nor can I envisage the once seats of petty Arab dynasties of

Petra, Palmyra, Edessa, Emesa and Hatra as conquering the world. This then is my secret torture – of coming to Britain by mistake – but I am hoping against hope that my interpretation of the Egyptian book of divination is wholly erroneous, especially as it foretells not only the end of the empire but of the whole universe.

The reasons of state for the expedition to Britain can be traced back to that cursed Albinus, who removed the British garrison to fight me in Gaul. Hadrian's wall was breached[10] and the northern barbarians, Caledonians and Maeatae, invaded the Roman province. I therefore came to Britain with a formidable army, my wife Julia and sons Antoninus and Geta and the whole court. I left Geta in London to administer the affairs of the southern province and to carry on the civil administration of the empire with a council of my senior officials[11]. Preparations for the expedition included supply lines and new granaries for the corn shipped from southern Britain and the Rhineland. To navigate the difficult British rivers, I brought Tigris bargemen from the new province of Mesopotamia who gave their name to the port of Arbiea,[12] from their name, Arab.

There were no real battles in the beginning, only skirmishes, as the enemy hid in the woods and marshes and the army spent its time cutting down forests, levelling hills, bridging rivers and draining swamps. The swamps caused great suffering to the soldiers who complained of chest pains and got stuck in the mud when they were often attacked. In such cases they were sometimes slain by our own men to avoid capture[13]. So far, in this second year of the campaign, 50,000 soldiers have already died, mainly from the severity of the winter march across the hills of Caledonia. The established pattern of this war has become surrender after a fierce battle, followed by short periods of pacification, then revolt. As the war dragged on, I became impatient and the soldiers restless, so I decided on a campaign of slaughter, quoting Agamemnon, 'Let no man escape utter destruction.'[14] I put my son Antoninus, who is already co-emperor, in charge of the campaign, but instead of advancing he tried to win the loyalty of the army by slandering his brother, and by characterizing me as a nuisance. He succeeded with a few soldiers who declared him sole emperor, deposing his crippled, bedridden old father. On hearing of the matter, I had myself carried to the tribunal and ordered all those responsible - tribunes, generals and cohorts - to be punished. When they begged for pardon, I touched my head and told them, 'Now you know the head does the ruling, not the feet.'[15] On the submission of the Caledonians and their surrender of substantial territory, Antoninus and I assumed the title of Britanicus and so did Geta, for Julia had succeeded after ceaseless pressure and taking advantage of my illness, in making me raise him also to the rank of Augustus and co-emperor. I had resisted her pleas on his behalf for a long time, fearing the consequences. Geta is, I know, only twelve months younger than his brother, but I waited twelve years to give him equal rank and now, after his elevation, I have the fearful certainty that Antoninus will kill him.[16] I am realising too late that my plans for the succession are less than wise. I have often blamed my adopted father Marcus Aurelius for his calamitous failure to remove his son, Commodus, from the succession, yet how many times have I threatened to remove Antoninus, without carrying out my threat? I am ashamed to admit in these memoirs that my love for my son has outweighed the love of my country, and in sparing my elder son I have betrayed the younger.[17] But above all, I am betraying the Empire that I have laboured for eighteen years to bring to this state of felicity, and in that I have betrayed myself.

The intrigue of my son with the army, among other reasons, has forced me to announce that I will take command of the spring campaign myself, and that I will lead the army from my litter, knowing full well that I will not actually be able to do so, but preparations have been long under way, for my plan is a permanent occupation of northern Britain. The marching camps built over a large part of Caledonian territory are nearly finished and are large enough to include the major part of the army of Britain, and stone fortresses with accommodation and baths have been built by the legions VI Vicrix and the II Augusta[18] as bases for our advance into hostile territory. Our push will start within days, which has necessitated the calling of a meeting of the war council. I have specifically asked for the fleet commanders of Britain, Germany, Pannonia and Moesia and the flotillas of the Rhine and the Danube to be present, for without their protection of the supply lines the campaign will be impossible. Also summoned are the official in charge of the granaries and the legates of all legions in Britain[19], the governor of Britain and Julia's Syrian clan of officials. In addition, Aemilius Papinianus (Papinian) the praetorian prefect, Julia's brother-in-law Julius Avitus Alexianus, his son-in-law the procurator of Britain Sextus Varius Marcillus of Apamea and the head of my secretariat will attend. The Council will decide on the date of our advance.

Talking of the campaign has made me forget that the key to this memoir was my dream, for I am a believer in prophetic dreams, portents, omens and oracles. The dream I had last night was not a rosy one like the dream I had three nights ago in which I was snatched up to heaven in a jewelled car drawn by four eagles and from there removed to the bosom of Jupiter and placed among the Antonines.[20] That was a happy dream of a longed-for death, an end to a vicious disease which hesitates in its course and crawls rather than runs. The slow pace is not to my taste, nor to the taste of the co-emperor, my son, who has been trying to persuade my doctors and attendants to hasten the process by poison.[21]

Last night I dreamed[22] I was walking in the woods which surround our camp. I was oppressed by the silence; no inhuman shrieks from the enemy in the depths of the marshes and forests beyond. More surprising still was the silence of our camp; no nostalgic guttural tunes from my Pannonian legions, no loud disputes from the Danubians, no soft tambourines from the Palmyran archers so far from home, no piercing wails from the Arabians who are always lamenting or just yearning for their desert tents, no voluptuous serenades from the Italians, no loud curses in dreadful camp Latin from the Gauls and no drunken brawls from the Goths. I must have lost my way in the woods; the mist was dense and the vapour filled my nostrils. Half shadows hovered around me as I struggled through entangled branches and an icy wind chilled my bones. I wrapped my shaggy woollen cloak around my shoulders and tried to extract my feet from the mud, and then I heard the hesitant footsteps of a man. From the way he shuffled his feet I could tell he was old. I strained my eyes through the fog and drizzle and saw standing some feet away the augur and senator Plautius Quintillus, my adopted brother-in-law, the son-in-law of Marcus Aurelius. I opened my lips to greet him, but then it dawned upon me that he was dead and that I stood censured for killing him by forcing him to take his own life.[23]

I was shaking; I, the master of thirty-three legions could not bring myself to face him. He stood erect despite his years and said slowly, shaking his finger at me, 'How dare you call yourself a son of Marcus Aurelius, an Antonine, while you are a usurper, an upstart, a superstitious cruel Punic alien?' He took a deep breath and went on, 'You wish to die but death avoids you. You are broken with grief and cannot support the pain.' And he laughed, the wind in the woods echoing his triumph. 'This is what I wished upon you when my soul was midway between the living and the dead. I asked for the same fate as Servianus asked for Hadrian[24], that you should wish for death but that death should elude you. My prayers have been answered, Severus: for the last two years your atrocious pain has made you long for death to no avail, but now I come to release you from my malediction and you know what that means.'

I started to speak, to tell him that I had had no hand in his death, that I never sent him word to take his own life but that I learned only too late what the speculators and *frumentarri*[25] had done, but my words were lost in the wind. He continued to rave like a madman. 'Severus, you long for death; why haven't you taken your own life? The divine Hadrian at least tried. He ordered his doctor to give him poison but the doctor refused and killed himself instead, but you cling to your crippled half-paralysed limbs. Your son Bassianus, whom you had the effrontery to rename Antoninus, will do the job for you. He tried to kill you in the presence of the legions and the barbarians, and at this very moment he is working hard at bribing the doctors to do away with you[26], but the gods will not grant you relief until you wish with all your heart that you had remained in Leptis, a nondescript Carthaginian among others, instead of masquerading in the purple as the first Roman!"

Quintillus paused but I remained speechless and he resumed. 'Tell me, pray, what was my crime in your eyes? The only intervention I made in the Senate was in your favour. Let me refresh your memory. You were marching to Rome with your Pannonians who declared you emperor. You disarmed your rival Clodius Albinus, governor of Britain, patrician-born member of the senate by naming him Caesar and promising him succession. His reputation in Rome was high[27] and you treated him with respect to ensure his neutrality while you fought your other rival Niger. The joke in Rome was that you wrote to him as "brother of your soul" and sent him Julia's salutations while we all knew that Julia's ambition would push you to repudiate him and elevate her son as Caesar. Albinus was vain and rather simple, and you flattered him by calling yourself an old man while he was still in the prime of his youth.[28] Your pretext for the march on Rome was to avenge the murder of the Emperor Pertinax, and as you claimed, to save Rome from Didius Julianus, who literally bought the empire from the praetorian guards. Pescennius Niger, the governor of Syria, had also let himself be declared emperor by his troops but unfortunately did not march on Rome, although the people were calling upon him to save them and to protect the empire from the outrageous Julianus. Nobody, I recall, asked you for help! Julianus declared you public enemy, but when he saw the Italian cities surrender with no resistance, and the senatorial delegation defect to you in Umbria[29], he started to pressure the senate to form another delegation which would include vestal virgins and the colleges of priests to plead with you to share the empire with him. I alone of the senators ridiculed the idea and stated bluntly that it would be impossible for us to convince you to desist from entering Rome[30]. I thus bought you a respite, and you entered Rome after a march you pursued by night and day in the midst of your soldiers who did not once take off their breast plates until they reached Rome[31]. You entered on foot in civilian attire with your men in full armour. The city offered you flowers and laurel[32] and was ablaze with torches and pungent with incense. We senators walked in state among citizens dressed in white.

'The second day you came to the senate where you passed a decree: "The emperor shall not be permitted to put any senator to death without consultation with the senate."[33] Don't you find that funny, Severus?' And he laughed a macabre laugh.

'Tell me, pray, how many senators did you put to death? The best part was that you executed the senator Julius Solon, who framed the decree for you.[34] Yes, you entered Rome with your barbarians with the ruddy faces, blond beards and curls, spreading terror and disgust amongst the population[35]. As if that were not enough, you disbanded the Praetorian guards, the pride of the empire, and replaced them with your barbarians. You dismissed the youth of Italy who turned to brigandage and gladiatorial fighting.[36] I left Rome for the country, for it was painful to me, as to other Romans, to hear savage dialects in the alleys of Rome and to see the barbarous lack of respect for our traditions and ancestral gods. But you the Cathaginian, who became Princeps, the first of the senate, and of the people, the incarnation of the law and guardian of the auspices, holder of the sacred title of Augustus; you who represented the imperial genius which bound the incongruous federation of cities in the east and west together in the universal empire (*orbis Romanus*)[37], did Roman tradition mean nothing to you that you trampled it so? Yes, Severus, I lived quietly until your spies informed on me. This was in your bitter years, after the murder of your beloved Plautianus. Before his death all your acts of cruelty were laid at his door. After that, the cruelty was yours alone. You were obsessed with secret plots against you and I was a victim of your dubious informers. I knew what that meant. I called for my funeral shroud which I had laid aside many years before, but I found it tattered so I cried to the gods, "What does this mean, are we late?" I burned incense, put on a new funeral shroud and opened my veins. I then wished on you what you are now: a lonely, sick old man whose ambition has given him nothing.' And with a chuckle, he vanished.

I stood shivering in the gloomy wood, my Roman identity shattered. The three centuries and a half since Carthage was destroyed by the Romans are not enough for old Quintillus. How dare he come from the dead to accuse me of his murder? I have committed and ordered countless deaths, for which I take full responsibility, but his murder I did not order. It was the informers, that obnoxious tribe which infests Rome and which takes part of the confiscated estate of the accused as a reward. I was shaking with indignation. Where would the senatorial aristocracy and their Roman traditions be if I had not preserved the State? I took over an empire burdened with foreign and civil wars, and I am leaving one in profound, universal and honourable peace.[38] I have erected more public monuments in Africa, Greece and Asia to the glory of Rome than any other emperor. I am the only emperor since Trajan who has extended the territory of the empire by adding a new province in the east. I forced the Parthians to retreat and sacked their capital.[39] Roman arms are once again supreme. My reign is the reign of the law, with jurists of world fame. I wonder who is more Roman, Quintillus with his lamentations over the good old days of Roman virtue and Roman tradition or I who made the subject peoples identify with Rome. And as for those romanised barbarians he derides, perhaps he forgot that they die every day on our frontiers to preserve the security of the empire.

I turned to leave, having extracted my feet from the mud. I was overcome with joy – I could move my feet and I could walk! And then I awoke from my dream to feel my feet heavy as lead as I lay paralysed on my bed with the sweat running through my hair, my beard and down my cheeks. Castor hurried in when he heard me groan. 'It is only a dream,' I said. I tried to raise myself, but I could not. 'Oh Hercules, Oh Jupiter, Oh Serapis, Oh Liber, Oh ye gods, I wish to die!' And suddenly I realised the significance of the dream. Old Quintillus came to tell me that his wish had been fulfilled and it was time for me to die. The gods had given me two clear indications in the short time left to me. First, the stars, under which I was born, and which I had painted on the ceilings of the rooms in the palace where I held court, except for the portion of the sky when I first saw the light. I allowed no one in that room, for it foretold the hour of my death. I therefore knew when I left for Britain that I would not return.[40] Old Quintillus confirmed it in my dream. It is time now for me to step out of the circle – where I have gone round and round to nowhere, and now detached from the wheel, reviewing as the Olympians, a life so distorted in the vision of others – both the living and the dead. I feel flat and empty, with no assumptions or delusions left, and yet I am guilty of retaining a lingering desire for the survival of this Antonine house which I have built with toil and blood. The continuing of the dynasty is essential for Rome and its mission to rule the world, and to bring Roman law and justice to all the peoples of the empire. The paradox, however, is that I have no doubts that the eternal Rome of Augustus and Antonius Pius will continue to rule the world for some time to come, but my hope for the survival of my house has been severely shaken by an oracle. Many years ago when I was a legate in Syria, I heard of the famous oracle of Zeus Belus, the god worshipped in Apamea, and that Trajan, before embarking on the Parthian war, sent to ask the oracle if he would return to Rome. The oracle sent him a centurion's baton broken into pieces and in less than four years the body of the emperor was returned to Rome in pieces.[41] I consulted the oracle again, which gave me this time a passage from Euripides: 'Your house will perish utterly in blood!'[42] Naturally, I have not revealed the prophecy until now - you can imagine how my enemies and my rivals would seize on it - but it has been on my mind all these years.[43]

The dream haunts me. Old Quintillus brought back distasteful memories of the disdain I had for my lords the *clarissimi*.[44] They accepted me by force of arms, and yet they felt threatened, for they recognised from the start that I would renounce the fiction of the constitutional principate instituted by Augustus, and that I was intent on absolute monarchy. They also felt threatened as I began to remove the ancient senatorial aristocracy and replace it by a new administrative equestrian elite.[45] Senators have been the plague of my life. It was hate at first sight. It all began with the murder of the Emperor Pertinax when the senator Julianus bid against another senator, Sulpicianus, city prefect and father-in-law of the assassinated Pertinax, for the empire. They bargained with the praetorian guards like fishwives, and the Roman Empire went to the highest bidder, Julianus[46] – an episode I labelled the most infamous and shameful in Roman history. It filled me with such revulsion that when I entered Rome after Julianus was murdered – by the soldier of whom he asked, 'But what evil have I done? Whom have I killed?'[47] I could only applaud the soldier's reply: 'You only killed Roman honour!'

So Julianus was executed by the soldiers and I in turn executed Sulpicianus. I proceeded to the Capitol and then to the palace, with the standards taken from the disbanded praetorians borne before me, not raised up erect but trailing on the ground.[48] I found the senate full of the partisans of Albinus whom I named Caesar, of Niger governor of Syria, who declared himself emperor in Antioch and had the support of the Roman populace. The Roman aristocracy closed ranks around Albinus although like me he was an African from Hadrumetum. I even encouraged him to strike coins as Caesar, which bore the legend Baal Hamon of Hadrumetum[49], advertising his African origin.

My act of self-adoption into the house of the Antonines in AD 195 after my first Parthian victory caused the senators great dismay.[50] They thought it was for vainglory and I never bothered to explain to them that it was rather an act of gratitude, for I owe the broad stripe on my toga – the sign of my new senatorial rank – and my posts in the service of the state to Marcus Aurelius, and to his son, Commodus. I loved and admired Marcus Aurelius. He was the idol and the ideal of my youth, but beyond the admiration and gratitude an unbroken and undisputed succession was imperative for the stability and unity of the Empire. From Vespasian to Commodus, seven emperors had succeeded legally for one hundred and ten years. Only Domitian was the victim of a revolution. This stability, after the chaos which had followed the extinction of the Julio-Claudian house, was mainly due to adoption.[51] Five emperors were adopted into Antonines and I didn't see why this policy should not continue, if it meant the preservation of the state. My adoption, however, was not only resented by the senate, but ridiculed by the people. Pollienus Auspex, governor of Lower Moesia, adored in Rome as the cleverest man at jokes and repartee and for despising all mankind, came to me after the adoption and said, 'I congratulate you, Caesar, upon finding a father!'[52] The insult, implying an obscure birth and an unknown father, had to be swallowed with a smile, for even the emperor could not afford to invite further enmity which would certainly result in an avalanche of even worse jokes.

The greatest revenge I had on their excellencies in the senate was the deification of Commodus, which I announced in a speech during which I watched their faces turning from red to black to green. I taunted them, and said that I deplored with them the disgraceful behaviour of my brother in slaying wild beasts in the arena with his own hands. I continued, 'Is it my imagination, or was it you who stood in that arena shouting, "You are lord and you are first. Victor thou art and victor thou shalt be!"[53] Yes, you stood and cheered him, and now you want to vilify him because he is dead! Have you not heard the saying, "Commodus was unpopular, only among the degraded"?'[54] Here I paused, and then, while their excellencies shuffled their feet nervously, I thundered, 'Was it not this august body that voted that the age of Commodus should be named the Golden Age and that this should be noted in all the records? Have you forgotten that you called Commodus Golden One and Hercules? And now you resent his deification, while in life you yourselves called him god?[55]

'No, no, noble fathers,' I said, unable to control my mockery. 'It does not befit you or your august office to apply a double standard, for you live worse lives than him. Only the other day in Ostia, one of your members, an old man, an ex-consul, was publicly sporting with a prostitute who imitated a leopard!'

Trouble for the senators came only after my defeat of Albinus when I eliminated all his supporters. Unfortunately for them, I had found their correspondence in his headquarters which, foolishly, he had not destroyed because he was sure of victory. I showed them the evidence of their treason during a speech in the senate; letters pleading with Albinus to come to Rome and rid them of the usurper! This while I was fighting Parthians in the east! Before I finished my speech, my soldiers arrested sixty-four senators of whom twenty-nine were executed.[56]

I still have mixed feelings about Albinus because I liked him and intended him to succeed if I was killed fighting Julianus or Niger.[57] I treated him as one would a son, but he was the initiator of the rift[58], for he sent troops to Gaul and declared himself emperor while I was on my way to Rome. I believe it was the title of Caesar conferred on my son Antoninus that caused Albinus to feel repudiated, though actually I gave that title under pressure from the army and from Julia, and did not mean to oust him from the partnership of the empire. I forgot that Albinus knew the ambitions of Julia for her sons, and knew her power. It is too late, alas, but what would I not give to have that gentle, vain, simple man alive to take the succession, instead of my violent, evil-minded son? I knew that the senate thought that I pretended to honour Albinus, so as to win him over and to keep him and his army quiet in Britain. But the truth was that not only did I like him but I needed a man of noble birth, still in his prime, while I was already an old man at forty-eight, wracked with gout, and my children still very young, I needed him so much that I even ignored rumours of Albinus' involvement in the assassination of Pertinax.[59] My triumph over Albinus at the battle of Lyon was a hollow victory indeed, for so many soldiers fell on each side that it dealt a severe blow to Roman power.[60] Albinus killed himself and I, by sending his head as a warning to the senators in Rome, showed a cruel anger, which I cannot justify.

My relations with their excellencies were now completely ruined, for I favoured the less wealthy, less powerful equestrians at the expense of the senatorial order.[61] I filled two thirds of the senate with eastern and Hellenistic senators.[62] Ironically, I an African, reduced the influence of Africans in the senate which had been so great under Aurelius and Commodus. I admit that I made an exception of my compatriots, the Lepticans, who I favoured not only in the senate, but also in my entourage. The composition of the senate was now one third Italians, instead of over half under the Antonines.

The senators had other grievances against me, and they never willingly accepted my laws on abortion, adultery and marriage[63]; nor my punishment of corrupt judges. My confiscation of senatorial property and that of governors and legionary legates, an aftermath of the civil war, was also very much resented. The estates of noblemen in Gaul and Spain, Syria and Africa who had opposed me went to the public treasury. I gave money to soldiers and have left a fortune to my sons and an enormous amount to the state, unlike any other Emperor before me. I was aware of the distress of families whose fortunes had been confiscated and in certain cases, when I was informed of the matter, I made restitution, as in the case of the daughter of senator Flavius Athenagoras, who could not marry because she had no dowry. I gave her a million sesterces from her father's estate[64].

Although I may sound bitter when speaking of the traitors and buffoons of the senate, I cannot deny the many remarkable men among them whom I openly admired. One of these, Erucius Clarus, was a noble Roman who upheld the traditional values that I so cherish. I sent him one of my freedmen with the promise that if he informed against those of his colleagues who were like him supporters of Albinus, I would pardon him. But Clarus preferred honour to life.

I must close my reflections on the senate on a positive note: the change in this august body has been very marked between the first and last years of my rule. They have learned to tolerate me, and now in the curia when they hear of the achievements of my governors and legates, they call, 'All do things well since you rule well.' But I cannot allow myself to take such cries seriously as I remember them shouting to Commodus, 'You are Lord, and you are first.'

In my old age I sometimes regret reducing the Senate to a servile role, but years of struggle and eighteen years of rule have brought me to the sad conclusion that the world is divided into elite and masses. For me, it is the military elite, for Julia it is the intellectual elite, for some it is the aristocratic elite. But my belief in an elite has not stopped me from sympathising with the oppressed masses. This sympathy for the downtrodden is the only trait which I have passed to my son Antoninus, who will continue my work for equality in the provinces. I have not created a utopia in my eighteen years of rule; it would have been more elegant if I had done so. But I say with pride that the Roman empire today offers to its sixty million subjects the greatest gifts that a state can grant: equity and justice based on humane laws, something the world has never known. This, I know, is not enough for philosophers, who dream of perfection beyond the scope of man but the world being as it is, I have played my small part in reshaping it.

SECOND NIGHT

Punica Fides

Eboracum (York)
30 January AD *211*

How often have I told my courtiers - hypocrites and servile idiots who flatter with their lips and curse me in their hearts - that I am not king of Rome, nor of Italy, nor a Latin tribal chief, for if I were, their resentment of a Punic provincial as their chief would be justified. But I *am* a Roman Emperor, the head of many peoples, races and nations; a Gaul, a Rhinelander, a Pannonian, Thracian or Egyptian has the same claim to my attention and concern as an Italian. I am the head of an empire which is the common country of many different nations. Rome has succeeded in subordinating many peoples, including my own, and governs them with a humanism shared with and adopted from Greece. It has established a superb military, administrative and judicial order acceptable to all those who are separated by history, culture and nationality. The idea of a worldwide imperial government was created by Augustus, forced on him by the conquests of Pompey and Julius Caesar and carried out by his successors in varying degrees. In other words, since Augustus the Roman people have been progressively denationalised. Needless to say, the imperial world government which deals with vast territories is not the same as the early republic[1] for which some Romans are nostalgic; they have not accepted that others may share the name Roman. To them, a descendant of Hannibal, the greatest enemy Rome has ever known, has become the master of

Rome. What sacrilege! This enmity has survived through three centuries, nurtured by writers and poets. Silius, who used Livy's book on the second Punic war as a source for his *Italicus Punica*[2], the longest epic in the Latin language, puts this into Hannibal's mouth: 'Rome, you may thank the wind and the stormy weather for a single day's reprieve, but tomorrow will never snatch you from my grasp, not if Jupiter descends to earth.'[3] The poet Statius in the *Silvae* describes Hannibal as 'Sidonian General, ruthless, treacherous and arrogant, hated by the gods as being drenched in Italian blood.'[4] Ironically, in the same book Statius dedicated an ode to his friend and fellow poet, my great-uncle and namesake Septimius Severus, in which he honoured him by rejecting his Punic origin. 'Your speech is not Punic, nor your dress, your mind is not foreign, you are Italian...Italian.'[5]

Juvenal, in one of his satires, shows admiration for Hannibal, but revels in his downfall. 'A fine sight it must have been, a fit subject for caricature - the one-eyed commander perched on his monstrous beast! Alas, alas for glory. What an end was here: the defeat, the ignominious headlong flight into exile.'[6]

This hate became part of the tradition as a nursery threat: '*Ad Hannibal ad Portas*' – Hannibal is at the door! Livy, the sober historian, in his *War with Hannibal*, was fascinated by the personality of this alien figure, his country's arch-enemy who was possessed of qualities he is compelled to admire[7], and paid him the highest praise any man can: 'Indeed I hardly know whether Hannibal was not more wonderful when fortune was against him, than in his hours of success.'[8]

Fortunately for Statius, he is not alive to see a Punic emperor on the throne, and not only that, but one who has retained a Punic accent[9] too harsh for the Latin ears of the *clarissimi*. I can still hear the faint sounds of suppressed laughter when I spoke to the senate. I would exaggerate my accent to see if anyone dared to laugh aloud instead of sniggering behind my back; and when my sister, Septimia Octavilla, came to visit me from Leptis, the injurious remarks reported to me on her heavy accent - for she could scarcely speak Latin - made me send her back, not because she embarrassed me, as they claimed[10], for I am absolutely careless of what is said about me[11], but because I was afraid of losing control of my temper if I chanced to hear their comments. So I resigned myself to their having a little fun behind my back.

Perhaps the one act that demonstrated to the whole Roman world how proud I was of my origins was that I rehabilitated the memory of Hannibal. I visited his unmarked grave in a place called Lebyssia where the vanquished hero took refuge with the King of Bithynia who betrayed him to the Romans. When Hannibal learned of this cowardly act he took his own life by poison. His tragic exile and death is best described by Juvenal: 'The once mighty Hannibal turned humble hanger-on, sitting outside the door of a petty Eastern despot till His Majesty deign to wake. No sword, no spear, no battle-flung stone was to snuff the fiery spirit that once had wrecked a world: those crushing defeats, those rivers of spilt blood were all wiped out by a ring – a poisoned ring.'[12]

I erected a white marble tomb over his grave[13] and inscribed it, 'To the greatest general of antiquity'. Hannibal was my hero, and for many years I believed I was his incarnation.[14] But with time I rejected the doctrine and now, on the threshold of death, I know better than to think that man has a thousand chances and a thousand lives ahead. Frankly, I cannot see further than this life, and in this I agree with my father who wrote in his meditations, 'Remember that no man loses any other life than this which he lives, nor lives any other life than this which he now loses.'[15]

It was vain of me to think that I could erase the perfidy attributed to Hannibal and, through him, to all our race, for how can one pluck from the tongues of Romans a favourite saying? They have transformed *bona fides* into *Punica fides*, a perjorative term meaning Carthaginian bad faith or treachery. The phrase is deeply embedded in Roman speech and has caused me endless mirth, especially when those talking to me say, *Punica fides* and then, realising their lapse, stop and stammer. I ignore their discomfort and say, 'Go on, you just said *Punica fides.*' White as a sheet, they stutter and beg my pardon and I dismiss the apology with a loud laugh. I was always proud of my family, but pride does not express the bond that ties me to my people and my landscape. It is a sort of possessive tribal feeling built on blood, and is somehow very Punic. It explains perhaps my two marriages and that of my son, to women of the same race. I did, however, succeed in transferring to the whole empire this tribal feeling, implanted in early childhood, and I became possessive of all its people and its various landscapes.

My paternal grandfather was a *duuvir*, a title which replaced the Punic title *sufete* (judge) which persisted until Trajan.[16] My father was a gentle man who had no political ambition and spent his time happily managing the family estates. My family had been Roman citizens long before my birth, not merely citizens, but equestrians before Trajan.[17] As to the antiquity of my race, my memories go far back to long winter evenings snuggled in my grandmother's lap by the hearth of our ancient house in Leptis. The house was falling apart and was full of draughts. My mother, who complained of chest pains, would start to cough and on the first sneeze my grandmother would order the brazier to be lit. I always loved that large bronze basin full of glowing charcoal. As the slave carried it to my mother's feet, I would slip from my grandmother's knee to sit beside her and hold my hands over the embers. My brother Geta used to kick me or pull my sister Octavilla's long plaits, and she would curse him aloud then stuff her mouth with figs and nuts.

When my mother saw my gaze fixed on the brazier, she always shuddered and cried, 'Lucius, don't, don't', for my fascination with fire goes back a long time. She would remind me how, as a baby, I thrust my hand into the glowing embers, and while they were busy putting ointment and bandages on my badly burned fingers, I put the other hand into the brazier. My mother said she had been frightened for me ever since; firstly because I did not cry, and secondly, because it revealed a foolhardiness, an obstinacy and a rashness. 'May the lady Tanit protect him, if he is so rash as a baby, what would he not do when he grows old!'

I remember too, my grandmother's stories, and one occasion in particular when she suddenly clapped her hands together and said in a raised voice, 'Lucius is the only one ready for my histories, for we have a long time before the evening meal.' That was an understatement. I was not only ready but had begged and pleaded with her for an hour to tell me tales. This made her indignant. 'Lucius, I never tell tales; this is history! For tales go to your Aunt Septimia Polla; the poor spinster lives on legends and tales!" My mother whispered from her corner, 'She lives on gold too, she is so rich!'

My grandmother ignored the acid remark and turned to me. 'Where shall we begin, child? Last time it was about Elissa Dido who founded Carthage.'

'You never told me why she burned herself,' I said, all excited.

'Ah, her tragic end. But she sacrificed, not burned, herself, Lucius,' my grandmother said. She sighed and continued. 'You know that her brother Pygmalion, King of Tyre, murdered her husband, and so she fled in a boat accompanied by Tyrian nobles, and landed on these Libyan shores by way of Cyprus, and after she had founded Carthage, the Libyan king asked for her hand. She refused, but the Tyrians, who needed an alliance with the natives, begged her to accept. She pretended to yield, but insisted on a ceremony before the marriage to release her from her promise to her dead husband. For the ceremony, she ordered a huge fire and threw herself into it.'

'Why, why?' I asked.

'She sacrificed herself for the prosperity of her people and their town. Later they deified her and her cult persisted until the fall of Carthage.'[18]

To the joy of my grandmother, I asked her whether Dido's sacrifice was the same as that of Abdmelquart Hamilcar, to which she answered, 'That was much later, child. You know that he was the grandfather of Hannibal and he went to fight in Sicily at Himera with an army of three hundred thousand men. During the battle he stayed in camp, trying from dawn till dusk to obtain a favourable omen from sacrifices. But as he poured the wine over the sacrificial victims he saw that his army was losing, so he ordered a fire and leapt into the flames, and was burnt to nothing.[19] The Carthaginians erected monuments to him in all their colonies.[20] Much later, his grandson Hannibal captured Himera and offered as expiatory victims three thousand prisoners at the place where Hamilcar sacrificed himself.'[21]

The question of human sacrifice tortured and frightened me. I knew that the subject of child's sacrifice was taboo but one night I dared to ask the question in a roundabout way. I pretended to cry and said, 'Grandmother, you know I am the first born. Would you have sacrificed me as a baby?' This question shocked my grandmother.

'Of course not, child. The Romans found the ritual barbarous and prohibited it.[22] But even before that many people used to sacrifice animals instead of babies.'

"But why did they do it?" I cried.

'Listen, child,' she said. 'In times of crisis – defeat in war, famine, flood or plague – people considered their misfortune to be a punishment from the gods. To appease the chief god, Baal, they confessed their sins and offered him the dearest thing they had in life, their babies. The richest and noblest families of the land had to set an example by offering their children first. They were obliged to assist at the sacrifice and were forbidden to weep or show their pain for they were renewing the divinity by blood.[23] The populace then followed their lead.'

Neither my grandmother nor the rest of the family had realised how troubled I was by the question of human sacrifice, and how my revulsion of that past practice made of me a fanatical Roman and a passionate advocate of Roman law.

It was from those winter evenings around the hearth that my zeal for just laws and my insatiable desire to delve into the Punic and Phoenician past grew. I pressed my tutors for information on Phoenicians which they could not give, but they did at least lead me to Herodotus, from whom I learned bits and pieces. In Herodotus I discovered that they settled in the Aegean on the island of Thera[24], that they circumnavigated Africa for an Egyptian king and that they introduced the letters of the alphabet to the Greeks.[26] As to their origins nothing satisfied me, so as my grandmother advised I went to my old maiden aunt Septimia Polla. 'Who are we, aunt,' I asked. Without hesitation she answered, 'Chanani.' That is Canaanites. When she saw my surprise and incomprehension she proposed that I accompany her to our estate, and there she told me to go and ask the villagers and peasants working on the estate who they were. I did, and the answer was always 'Chanani.'[27] I did not rest until I found out who those Canaanites were, and why they were subsequently called Phoenicians. I discovered that the name 'Phoenician' had been given by the Mycenaean Greeks to the Canaanites, who came into contact with them in the second millennium BC. Later, the term was confined to those Canaanites who lived on the coastal belt and retained their independence.[28] The origin is the Greek word *phoenikes*, which denotes dark red, purple or brown. The Greeks applied it to the brown-skinned Canaanites[29] or possibly to the purple dye they produced. The Roman name *Poeni* for the Canaanites of the west is a latinised version of the Greek word. The Canaanite homeland was Palestine and coastal Syria where they founded city states, but in the thirteenth century BC they were pushed back from the south by the Hebrews and Philistines. In the north, they were hard pressed by the Aramaens, but the Canaanite culture survived in its purest form on the coastal plain in the cities of Tyre and Sidon, and in the colonies established by them in the western Mediterranean, most famously Carthage.[30] Then Rome entered the arena, and the Punic wars began. Carthage was finally sacked by Scipio Aemilianus in 146 BC and remained in ruins until the Romans rebuilt it a hundred years later.[31] In the African territories annexed by Rome, Phoenician communities like Utica, Hadrumetum and Leptis had almost complete independence. They co-existed with the empire, their institutions were recognised and Leptis was called a 'friend and ally' of Rome. They were administered by their own *sufetes* and their priests (*kohanim*) stayed in their temples.[32]

By a twist of fate, it is in the colonies that the Phoenician language has survived and is still spoken today; in its homeland, after the conquest of Alexander in 322 BC, it died out and gave way to Aramaic, the language of the people, and to Greek, the official language and that of the upper classes.

In 47 BC Julius Caesar reduced the Punic territories from semi-independence to subordinate status and mergedOea, Sabratha and Leptis into what is now called Tripolis. Leptis was granted citizenship by Trajan. It was against this background that I grew up in a Leptis that, although recently Romanised, was full of Punic inscriptions on public monuments offered by men with Punic names – Annobel, Iddabaal, Ben Hanno, Abdmelquart – the last two recalling Baal and Melqart[33], the great Punic gods. But the town itself had taken on a Roman appearance with theatres, forum, circus and baths, and the Lepticans were beginning to change their Punic names for as citizens they had a legal right to Roman ones.

As Emperor, I granted *Ius Italicum* to Leptis, Carthage and Utica, giving them, in other words, the same privileges as Italian towns.[34] I remodelled part of Leptis, built a new harbour and enlarged the city's water supply. I added a colonnaded street, running from the baths, past the Severan basilica and the new forum, to the nympheum. A quadruple arch was built at the main crossroads. I imported architects and stonemasons from the east and instructed them to build in the Greek style rather than the Roman.[35] I commissioned sculptors to embellish the whole town; in fact, I beautified the city with buildings and monuments on a magnificent scale unparalleled in Africa. Leptis and Sabratha responded by dedicating numerous statues to me and to my family. Twelve statues were dedicated to me in the theatre of Sabratha. In Leptis, statues were erected in the theatre and in the baths and were dedicated to my parents, to my first wife and to my aunt, Septimia Polla.[36]

What a pleasure it was for me to see the provinces of Africa and Syria grow rich. With riches came splendour, but how fragile is all this magnificence! So much depends on the *limes*, the lines of defence with garrisoned forts. In Africa I extended the frontier, built the *Limes Tripolitanis*, and reconstructed the headquarters of the legion III Augusta in Lambaesis[37] to keep the savage tribes from sacking and plundering the cities. I did the same in the province of Arabia, with Roman limes stretching over the desert frontier to repel bedouin attacks. Later I repaired the wall of Hadrian in Britain, and went beyond it to pacify the barbarian tribes to keep them from attacking the frontier.

I have spent my life trying to stem the tide of barbarism in the eastern and western provinces, but for how long? In my heart I know that the ebb and flow, the cyclical nature of things will render these glorious Roman cities as nought. Wild growth and bushes will crack the marble in the basilica and the nympheum of Leptis, and the arch dedicated to me will be no more than a heap of rubble.

Speaking of Africa and Africans, many people attribute the sudden vertiginous rise of Africans to high positions to me, but this is a misconception. It was the three Antonine emperors before me who initiated the policy of conciliating the African elite, making them legates, magistrates and prefects. The African grouping in the senate rivalled the French and Spanish parties. But even before the Antonines some Africans had risen to power, among them literary men like Suetonius Tranquillus the biographer of the Caesars and chief secretary in Hadrian's reign, who was from Hippo Regis. It was my great uncles who paved the way for my first successes, and Laetus, was the first African praetorian prefect under Commodus[38]; but let no man think that I ascended the throne on a bed of roses. True, I believed that it was providence that called me to rule, but it was my own efforts that gave providence a hand!

My rise to power was well prepared. Having become proficient in Greek and Latin, I studied law in Rome and then acquired the post of *fisci advocatis*, pleader for the treasury, a relatively new office established by Hadrian.[39] Then I became quaestor in Baetica, Sardinia and Sicily. In Sardinia I spoke Punic to the inhabitants. The language was still in use and Punic influence was dominant.[40] To my great joy and due to the influence of my great uncle with the Emperor Marcus Aurelius, I received the broad stripe and was called to the senate.[41]

Needless to say, I felt exalted to enter that venerable assembly and to be called *vir clarissimus*. I received from the Emperor Commmodus[42] my first consulship, with Ruffines as a colleague, and the command of legion IV Scythica, stationed in Syria. Soon, however, Commodus became suspicious and wrote to Albinus in Britain that he didn't trust me, and I was discharged.[43] The murder of Commodus and the appointment of Pertinax led to my reinstatement. In the midst of my career, I felt restless. I had overtaxed myself and I was at the end of my youth. My family insisted that it was time to get married within the family circle in Leptis. They prevailed upon my great uncle C. Severus who was then pro-consul of Africa to bring me home. He complied with their request and appointed me *legati pro paetore*, tribune of the plebs. The position, I'm ashamed to say, went to my head to such an extent that when an acquaintance, a plebeian, embraced me on the street with the fasces being carried before me, I had him beaten and proclaimed, 'Let no plebeian embrace without due cause the legate of the Roman people!'[44] What an arrogant, pompous youth I must have been!

This rather glib review of some events in my career makes it seem smooth. It was not; there were always flies in the ointment. To my great embarrassment I was accused of adultery in Africa and treason in Sicily, and taken to court twice. In Leptis, as tribune of the plebs and before I married Paccia Marciana my first wife, I was accused[45] by a vicious dullard not of being his wife's lover, but of helping her to prevent his squandering of her dowry. It was folly on my part to play into the hands of this beautiful woman, whom I cannot in all honesty call a courtesan even though she had a long succession of lovers for, unlike a courtesan, she fell in love with every one of them! Her wealthy equestrian family disapproved of her conduct and severed all contact with her, but her husband was happy to close his eyes as long as he enjoyed her money. Drusilla, for that was her name, caught me unaware. She came into my office one day, resplendent in her silks and jewellery, and asked me with downcast eyes if I remembered her. She reminded me that I used to play judge and hold court with all the boys of the neighbourhood in attendance, and that she stood with the other girls watching me shyly from afar. She knew from my reputation that I was an excellent jurist, and she, a woman boycotted by her family for reasons of inheritance, neglected and cheated by her husband, sought my advice and help. Would I not rescue a defenceless woman? I was dazzled and fell. I believed her lies, until a relation of mine explained the reason for her family's boycott, even naming her many lovers some of whom I knew. When I faced Drusilla with this information she smiled and said gently, 'I was planning to tell you all but I could not shock you from the start, for

I sensed you were a prude!' Her frankness enchanted me and the stories about her lovers amused me greatly, for each one was the great love of her life until the next. 'You know, Lucius,' she told me one evening in a grove scented with carnations under the African moon, 'some women have sex appeal, but I have cad appeal; for I have managed to attract all the cads of Leptis, including thieves and perverts, and fall in love with each and every one of them. Oh, Lucius, Lucius, my dear, why did I never, never fall in love with a decent honourable man?'

I had to laugh but was indignant that she didn't consider me either decent or honourable. I told her, 'Drusilla, don't be confused, for in real love there must be honour.' And she cried and cried, for those whom she loved had in reality trampled her honour into the dust. In truth, she was a beautiful, sensual but simple, woman with a large heart. Her husband was very accommodating and insisted that I go to their house every night, but he became furious when my financial advice took effect. Lovers were permitted the use of his wife as long as he controlled her money. She began to annoy him with her demands that he account for lost sums and, incensed, he went before the magistrate to accuse me of adultery. I was lucky to be a trained jurist, and in defending myself I made mincemeat of the foolish man, bringing as witnesses her former lovers who stated that he had known but turned a blind eye to their relations with his wife. I was acquitted but never forgot Drusilla, and it was thanks to her that one of my first decrees as emperor protected women's dowries from their husbands by making the money returnable to them intact in full in the case of divorce. The severity of this law gave rise to much disgruntled criticism throughout my reign, but that scene in the Leptis court haunted me and I did not relent.

The second accusation, in Sicily, was much more serious. I was indicted for consulting with seers and astrologers about the imperial dignity, a treasonable crime punishable by execution. Commodus was detested, and had become suspicious of legates like myself whom he thought were ambitious for the throne. My legal training and reputation again proved valuable, and I defended myself to the prefects of the guards who acquitted me. My accuser was crucified.[46] It was true, of course, that I had been consulting with astrologers – I always have done – but I was not seeking to know about the Emperor's death. Oh yes, I was ambitious, but I knew I still had a long way to go before I could aspire to the throne.

After a year's interruption for study in Athens my career resumed; I was appointed by the new Emperor Pertinax governor of Upper Pannonia, where I had three legions at my command. My brother, Geta, received Lower Moesia with two legions, my future rival Albinus in Britain had three legions, and Pescennius Niger received the most important military post in the Empire, the governorship of Syria with three legions. Thus the stage was set for the civil war which followed.

When the civil war was over and I had defeated Julianus, Niger and Albinus, I was free to change the make-up of the empire and to strike a balance between the provinces and Italy. The Romans see themselves as conquerors and the provinces as inferior subject peoples, but the subject nations in the east – Asia, Syria, Egypt, Mesopotamia and Africa – can truthfully boast of being heirs to civilisations much more ancient than Rome. The Western provinces on the other hand had different problems, for they were being Romanised and were quickly moving from barbarism to civilisation. Consciousness of my origins caused me to seek a balance between the provinces and the privileged position of Italy. The praetorian guard, thus far an Italian preserve, was opened up to the courageous and talented from all provinces. I did not reduce the status of Italy, as some have claimed; I only raised the provinces to equal status.

By these measures, the future of the Empire was assured and the loyalty of the provinces to the emperor in Rome was strengthened, though I could not avoid Italian resentment.

They kept seeking new grounds to attack me: they called me the African Sulla, and took exception to my Syrian connection through the empress. It is true that I appointed and promoted many Syrians, some of them from Julia's friends or from her clan; but that was nothing new for when I came to power many high positions of state were held by prominent Syrians, and Levantine legates, sophists, teachers, writers and jurists were everywhere. My adopted father married one of his daughters to a Syrian who had been influential long before the Africans.

Julia, however, reacted to the situation differently. She lost her customary coolness and was greatly embarrassed, for she had assumed that her supposed 'royal origins' made her immune from attack, and that it was my African equestrian origins that were the target. One evening she burst into my office, fuming. 'Did you hear what they are saying in the drawing rooms of Rome? They are reciting the satire of Juvenal: "This mud-laden torrent pouring from the Orontes into the Tiber"[47]. And listen, there's worse. "It has caved to the language and customs of Syria the players of flutes and harps and exotic tambourines and the girls near the circus go to them. You who love barbarian mud."[48] They dare vilify us and call your wife Syrian mud while you do nothing about it.'

'My dear,' I replied sarcastically, 'I am touched by your fury; a solicitude I did not see when they were – and still are – calling me dreadful names, the African Sulla being the least of them. And have you forgotten the *Punica Fides*? What exactly do you have in mind? Do you want me to prohibit the Romans from quoting Juvenal, the greatest satirist in Roman history? Have you forgotten that I am a Roman Emperor and that you, a Roman Empress, should venerate him too?'

She turned pale and turned to leave the room. 'No, Julia,' I said. 'An empress does not run away. Didn't you know that Juvenal wrote that satire long before we came to Rome? And didn't you know, incidentally, that the city is full of houses of pleasure and that many of the girls are from Syria? They say that Romans prefer girls from Syria.' She was obviously shaken but I continued, 'Do you seriously think that I don't know what they are saying in their drawing rooms or know of their comments about your Syrian in-laws? I have detailed reports, my dear; informers are plentiful in Rome. Let them talk and pour out their resentment, as long as it is only in words.'

'I congratulate you, my lord,' Julia said in a raised voice, 'on your calm when it is a question of maligning your wife. I have seen you in a very different mood when you yourself were the target. Forgive me for disturbing you.' And she left.

'Raise the question in your sophist circle. A very good subject for debate!' I shouted after her. But Julia was right; I was not so calm when the rabble stealthily in the night painted the sign of Tanit – an esoteric triangular figure used in the worship of Baal [49] – on the bases of my statues and on the doors of public and private buildings in the alleys of Rome. I suppose I was more saddened than angry, for I had done so much for the underprivileged and the poor. I never ceased distributing money to them and laying on spectacles for their entertainment. Did this mob, revelling safely all night in the taverns of Rome, realise what a state they would be in if I had not brought law and order to the city or cleared Italy of brigandage? They would not otherwise have dared leave their houses at night! Some of the graffiti artists were caught and punished by the secret police who infiltrated their ranks, but it wasn't much of a consolation.

Sometimes I reflect on the laws of destiny and wonder how the world would have been had Carthage triumphed over Rome. It amuses me to think of Baal lording it over the Capitol, in a Canaanite empire. And I apply the same question to my own case: what if Niger or Albinus had won the civil war and resided in the Palatine Palace? What if it were my head instead of Niger's that was sent to Byzantium? Or my head instead of Albinus' that was sent to the senate in Rome?

How frail is the dividing line, how vague the demarcation between light and shadow, between success and failure. Does the answer lie in Roman courage versus Carthaginian weakness, or my efficiency versus my rivals' indolence? Does the fate of Carthage and Rome or Severus, Niger and Albinus make any difference to the myriad worlds in which our fate is ordained and written in the stars long before we were born?

THIRD NIGHT

Julia, Goddess of the Moon

Ebroracum (York)
31 January ad 211

The whole world loves my wife; I am the only exception. But what I feel for her, though not as great as love, is the next best thing: admiration and respect. I bestowed upon her a title which my father, Marcus Aurelius, gave to the Empress Faustina, *Mater Castrorum*. As such she is worshipped by soldiers and has become in her lifetime the object of a cult in Leptis as patron of two curias, Curia Augusta and Curia Julia, who have honoured her with inscriptions as *Mater Castrorum* and *Mater Augustrorum*.[1] She has become identified with Juno Caelestis, goddess of the moon, and the Punic goddess Tanit.[2] She appears with me on a new coin with the attributes of the sun and the moon, with the legend *Concordiae Aeternae*. Some talk of her beauty but, frankly, it is not to my taste, for her features are heavy and her eyes too large, probably due to Aramaen ancestry in her Arab blood. She doesn't have the delicate features of my beloved first wife, Paccia Marcia, nor the sensuality of Drusilla, nor indeed the Greek features of Penelope my love from Aphridsias who revealed to me in the flesh the figure I have only otherwise seen in statues of goddesses.

To be fair, I didn't marry Julia for her beauty, nor for her royal horoscope as they claim[3], but for her erudition, her intelligence, her haughtiness and her breeding. Julia and I have one thing in common: we are both alien to Rome. I never felt at home in Rome. I stayed there intermittently and only when my obligations required it. During the last years before I came to Britain, I moved with my family to the imperial property on the coast of Campania[4].

Emperors with simple tastes like Trajan and myself who hate ceremony and ostentation and the pampered splendour which surrounds the court, have the recourse of running to the camps and battlefields at the furthermost corners of the Empire. For me, this was always the best escape from palace protocol which I loathed. It was a nightmare to be woken by my Greek valet with his supercilious smile, demanding to know which outfit was required that day: palace clothes, city clothes, military uniform, full dress parade uniform or perhaps the *gladiatori* vest for the theatre? Each of these outfits had a special slave. They were followed by the specialist of the eating vessels. 'Caesar, are the silver or gold vessels required today? Shall we put out the rock crystal vessels encrusted with precious stones for the dinner in honour of the King of Armenia?' My answer was always the same. 'Go to the Empress. She will decide.' This was followed by a stream of slaves: first the one in charge of ornaments, pins and pearls, then the masseur, then the hairdresser.[6]

The hairdresser was the only one I could tolerate, for he arranged my coiffure in the Marcus Aurelius philosopher style or the Serapis style, depending on the fashion. When the major-domo responsible for meals came, I took pleasure in ordering my native African beans, without meat, and a little wine.[7] He met this with open contempt and complete dismay. I could see his lips moving with words he dared not utter: 'Can you believe it, an emperor who still thinks he is in camp, ordering food fit only for slaves.' I took pity on him and told him to go to Julia, for I relinquished all questions of protocol to her. I knew that she loved to discuss palace menus and delicacies with him. Julia loves pomp, ceremony and ritual. She also loves fine food, which she would order in quantity; stuffed quails, bird tongues, meats with thousands of sauces and fish which the chef adorned like works of art. She, like all Syrians, has a sweet tooth and orders marzipan and fruits in rose water almost daily.

I used to give instructions not to be disturbed in the morning for I would wake before dawn to look into whatever urgent demands lay on my side table from the previous night. Then I would take a walk with my officials to hear reports from the provinces, after which I held court at the palace where I judged lawsuits until noon. This was followed by a ride or gymnastics, a bath and lunch alone or with my sons, and then a nap and back to work.[8] Later I would have a walk, discussing philosophy, music, oratory or poetry, in Greek or Latin[9], with those of my companions or officials who had such interests. I rarely invited guests for dinner, and gave banquets only when it was unavoidable[10]. There is nothing that disgusts me more than the gluttony displayed at these banquets, and if I became estranged from Plautianus, it was because of his eating, drinking, vomiting, and eating all over again. He tried carefully to hide his gluttony, knowing how sparing I was in diet, but I once saw him devour sheep intestines roasted on charcoal with such relish that I forbade him to eat in my presence again. It was then that I realised there must be some truth in the reports of his sexual appetite too; the same lack of inhibition, decency and decorum as in his eating habits! As for clothes, I dismissed all the specialist slaves who had a costume for every occasion and retained my plainest clothes. My tunic had scarcely any purple and I covered my shoulders with my shaggy old cloak.[11]

My frugal habits in food and drink, my austerity in clothes and my hatred of ceremony were a constant source of friction between me and Julia. I accused her unfairly of ostentation and she accused me of rustic provincialism and of playing into the hands of our detractors; according to her, because we are both aliens in Rome, we ought to be more imperious than other emperors and empresses. She reminded me that *plebs* and aristocrats alike, love spectacles and that we have to provide them with a show of luxury and majesty. She craved jewels and loved to exhibit the enormous rubies and emeralds inherited from her father; I also indulged her with bigger and bigger emeralds, for that was her stone. She believes in the healing power of gems, especially for restlessness and mental illness, so that I could tell her psychic state from the jewels she wore. She was more sensitive than I to the subtle snubs of the conservative Roman aristocrats, and Julia's Arab pride would not accept humiliation. She has an innate superiority that nothing can shake, for in an Arab tribe, she tells me, every individual regards himself as equal if not superior to the chief. This belief, implanted in me by Julia's ceaseless repetitions, proved to be my Achilles heel, for I spared the Arab priest kings of Hatra through not wanting to place a yoke upon such a noble race and I called off the siege, a huge mistake.

But Julia's pride is excessive, especially when she looks down her long princess's nose with such disdainful haughtiness. She a princess of Emesa and I am nothing but a Roman legate who ended up as emperor. She does not allow anybody to forget – Jupiter! How boring that can be – that her dynasty have ruled Emesa as priest kings since the end of the Seleucid Era. She would turn to the aristocratic Roman ladies come to pay their respects, saying that her people obtained Roman citizenship more than two centuries ago, not like some people she knows; looking pointedly at those proud ladies whose families mounted the social ladder merely fifty or one hundred years ago. Her ancestors, she reminds them, proved their loyalty to Rome in the Parthian war and later in the war of Vespasian and Titus against the Jews. They furnished the Roman legions with archers and cavalry[12]. She quotes Cicero, who as governor of Cilicia wrote to her ancestor Jamblichus, the ruling priest king of Emesa and called him 'Phylarch of the Arabs and friend of our republic'.[13] Augustus installed them as petty princes, and the Emessene dynasty intermarried with the Herodian royal house[14], who were Edomites forcefully converted to Judaism by the Macabees, as were the Galileans. Each conquered people produced a notable Jewish leader who was not originally a Jew: Herod the Great was an Edomite from the south of Palestine who became King of the Jews, and the Galilean prophet Jesus, founder of the new religion Christianity.

This cult of Christianity is spreading like wildfire and must be checked. It is subversive and dangerous to Rome. The calculating Christians have fixed their sights on converting the high officials of state and even the household of the emperor. They went as far as to circulate rumours that Julia was an adept of their creed[15], all because she once hired a Christian nurse for Geta. The Romans knew better, however, for her zeal in the worship of the ancestral gods is much appreciated, along with her total indifference to the betyle[16], the conical stone idol of Emesa. Anyway, she is too intellectual for Christianity which she found very primitive. It was well known that she was enthusiastic about the cult that arose around 'Apollonius of Tyana'. She was, and still is, promoting the cult by all means possible, and has requested the writer Flavius Philostratus, a member of her salon, to write an account of his life. I confess that I am fascinated by this Apollonius and have never stopped quizzing Philostratus about him, for apparently he has healed the sick, raised the dead and ascended bodily into heaven[17]; the same, I am told, as did the founder of the new Christian religion. All these mystic cults plaguing the empire undermine the Roman religion, which has so far resisted but for how long?

I received alarming reports about the spread of Christianity. The Christians did not stop at Julia; they were also aiming at me. Tertullian, a compatriot from Carthage, and well versed in jurisprudence, was converted, and embarked on a new literary career. Three years ago, he submitted to me his *Apology* which explains his new faith and which I read with pleasure; for contrary to other tracts on his religion, the *Apology* is judicial in form and restrained in expression. The old fox knew I would read it because he tried to hide, but in vain, the contempt with which Christianity regards the Roman state. He asserts that 'it is a fundamental human right, a privilege of nature, that every man should worship acccording to his own conviction!' This was a direct attack on Scapula, my pro-consul in Africa, for his persecution of the Christians.[18] I asked jokingly, 'Are you trying to convert me, Tertullian?' 'No, Caesar. I have no hope that way. I submitted it to you in your capacity as a fellow African and a fellow jurist!' Cunning fox! But Tertullian's logic deserted him when he published his treatise *On the Dress of Women*. It caused such an uproar among upper-class ladies that I asked for Julia's opinion. She retorted, 'I have other things to discuss with my sophists than women's dress.'

Chrisitianity attracts the sub-strata of society, women and slaves. It could be regarded like any of the other cults of the empire but for the fanaticism and exclusiveness which it has inherited from its parent religion, Judaism. It refuses to acknowledge Roman gods or any other gods, unlike the 'Fellowship of Isis', with which it has much in common. The followers of Isis retain their existing obligations to the gods of their home and country. Isis and Jupiter co-exist.[19] The Roman gods are tolerant; they have assimilated with the gods of the Greeks, Egyptians, Phoenicians, Syrians and Arabians. But Christianity seeks exclusiveness; it wants to force itself alone on the the empire. A cult so un-Roman, with its subversiveness, its love feasts, its stress on suffering and martyrdom, makes me shudder at the thought that it may one day dominate. May the gods forbid it becomes an upheaval of our world so great that it brings it to an end. I therefore issued an edict just before the secular games forbidding conversion to Judaism or Christianity[20] and prohibiting all Christian missionary activities. I had not shown any hostility towards the Christians or Jews until this edict. The court physician is a Christian and many of my entourage are secret adherents, but now I am blamed for instigating a new persecution.[21] Reports from Alexandria say that the edict has borne fruit as Clement, the head of the Christian catechetical school, has quit both his missionary activities and Alexandria.

The edict has reminded the people of the empire that the Roman Emperor is the *Pontifex Maximus* and that tolerance has its limits. It may be argued that the cult of Mithras has spread in the army and is officially tolerated by the state, but it does not stop the soldiers from worshipping the Roman gods, their legionary insignia and deified emperors. Romans are free to worship the gods they please, as long as these gods are identified and assimilated into their ancestral gods. I, like my brother Commodus before me[22], am an adept of Serapis, the Greco-Egyptian god identified with Jupiter, whose ritual cult enacts death and resurrection, assuming both roles of the underworld and heaven. As a devotee of Serapis, I have taken the cult as a symbol of the dynasty implying eternal life. The legend which I have stamped on the coins, *aeternit temperi*, is the promise of a new golden age. I have requested the artists to make my portrait in the guise of Serapis with four hanging locks and a forked beard, the first such portrait was made in Egypt. What amazes me is the Christian belief that they have a monopoly on 'resurrection'; the idea is as old as time. The Egyptian god Osiris was resurrected and so was the Canaanite-Phoenician god Tamuz.

The story of Tammuz-Ashtar was transformed by the Greco-Roman world into Venus-Adonis. Ashtar was associated with Venus, and Tammuz became Adonis. This legend has taken hold of people's imagination to such a degree that I have seen it carved on marble sepulchres all over the eastern part of the empire, especially in the Greek cities of Asia and Syria. It is depicted on graves to prove that love is greater than death. I have been touched by the beauty of these reliefs which show Venus holding her wounded lover in her arms before he enters the underworld. The anonymous sculptors have caught her pain and anguish so entirely that it comes through the cold marble. Adonis dies but returns in spring, a resurrection following the natural cycle of the seasons. This carving in marble, with images of blood, death and resurrection on the tombs was also carried to the theatre of Volupte and death in pantomimes. I have seen the same spectacle in the Saturnalia given by Syrians and Phoenicians, with Venus represented in mourning when the solar cycle goes to the lower hemisphere, as if the sun is lost forever, but returns after a temporary death[23]. Looking at these reliefs on so many graves, I feel such pity for man who is forever seeking consolation when there is no consolation for death. And I, a dying man, attempting in these memoirs to find some perspective on my life, neither seek nor find any consolation. I stop dictating every now and then because a landscape fixes itself in my vision:- a grove of green ferns near a spring of running water, a terraced slope overlooking the sea, or a mound in the desert where in the cool evening the stars are so bright, snow falling around the camp in Pannonia, not white but silvery in the grey twilight, or here in York where the wind rises suddenly with such clamour, such vengeance. It is not people I regret leaving behind, it is landscapes. If only I could carry with me across the Styx an image of a flowing river, the shade under an oak tree, a shelter in a raging storm. How I love storms, for truly in all nature they are my element.

I am digressing from Julia. I visited Emesa before I married her when it had become part of the Roman province of Syria, and found it less hellenised than the Phoenician coastal towns of Aradus, Tripolis, Byblos, Beyritues, Sidon and Tyre, where the Greek language became the official language and the Phoenician was supplanted by Aramaic, the *lingua franca* of all Syria. Arab Emesa considered itself Phoenician too, and its novelist, Heliadorus called himself 'Phoenician from Emesa from the race of the sun'.[24] Our similar backgrounds are a bond between Julia and me. She understands my Punic and I understand her Aramaic. However, we converse mainly in

Greek for she has a mastery of the language. Julia has one great love – call it an obsession – and it is not philosophy as she would have people believe, but power, and power jumped into her lap, or so she thought when I ascended the throne. She never dreamed when she left Syria and sailed to marry the governor of Lyon that she would become empress and the first lady of Rome. Her hunger for power was such that she acted as if it were her right to share in the government of the empire and, according to Plautianus, one would think that she had inherited the throne! However, she was not aware of my concept of government and did not know that I would totally reject her interference. I thwarted her attempts to be a Livia who assisted Augustus establish the empire, or a Plotina who helped Trajan in its consolidation. She even tried to play the princess role with me, but I told her plainly that she could go back to her hopping dancing priest of a father and rule with him the narrow strip that surrounds his temple. I never revealed my plans nor consulted her, except when she accompanied me to Syria, her home country. There she acted as my advisor, and her personal knowledge enabled me to understand the inner workings of the region, its rivalries, centres of power and intrigues. But although I kept Julia way from the source of power, I gave her all the honours due to a Roman empress and much more.

She appears with me on coins, portraits and statues, and shared most of my public appearances. Early in our marriage and long before she had her literary salon, she presided over the social scene in Rome and took it upon herself to clarify, justify and establish our posthumous adoption into the house of Antonines. Her conversation charmed, fascinated and even bewitched her visitors, whom she told repeatedly that my great-great adopted grandfather, Hadrian's father, was called Afer and was of African origin like myself, and Hadrian's mother was from Gades, the most ancient Phoenician centre in Spain. The sanctuary of Gades she explained, had conserved until the present the

Punic ritual. Its shaven headed priests were strictly continent; pigs and women could not enter the temple. The entrance has two columns of bronze, gold and silver which dazzle seamen with their brilliance, for the temple was visible far out at sea.[25] For Julia, this led to the certain belief that the two columns were really two betyles, the same as her native betyle in Emesa. Thus she associated us with Hadrian and made him of African Punic origin, like myself. Meanwhile, she never failed to remind her listeners that Antoninus Pius was from Provence, and the empress Plotina, Trajan's wife, was from Nimes; provincials like us!

To Julia's credit, she typified what the Romans expected from an empress. Talking of credits, I owe Julia a great deal. She introduced me not only to Syria but also to Arabia, and tried to satisfy my curiosity about the hidden, and beyond. From her I learned that the Greeks said that the Arabs worshipped stones, like the betyle. Further, that Doussara the great god of the Arabs, is the name of the highest peak in Arabia. The Nabataean Arabs carried his worship to the islands of Cos and Delos and to Pouzzoles and identified him with Zeus.[26] Doussara, like El-Gabalus, had a solar function. The Arabs celebrated his birth on 25th December and regarded him as a son of a virgin named Khabou. Julia told me that the betyle or stone was worshipped in other Arab towns: in Adraa where the coins show a rounded block of stone and in Bosra, the capital of the province of Arabia, where the betyles are similar to the one in Emesa with a sun disc in the middle.[27] Julia was nostalgic about our time in Syria, for Syria had a special claim on me as her native land and I showered privileges on her cities. But that was the happy period of our marriage, for the war between her and Plautianus, my kinsman and praetorian prefect who had accompanied us, had not yet started. The people of Emesa were proud of their empress and used to give her great receptions with flowers, flutes and trumpets; her family would cover her with jewels as she played the role of Roman Empress and Queen of the Orient with imperious grace. She accompanied me once to Tyre, a pilgrimage to the home of my remote ancestors. Even now I find it difficult to express how I felt. It was as if time had stopped and I had returned home.

Before I left Syria I divided it into two regions, a measure against ambitious governors and future rebellions. I like to look back on that time, for the reorganization of Syria and the resumption of trade after the two Parthian campaigns brought prosperity and with it new public buildings. I put many Syrian families on the roster of Roman senators, beginning with Julia's family. I raised her brother-in-law, Alexianus, from the equestrian to the senatorial order and did the same for the husbands of her nieces, Maesa's daughters.[28]

The annexation of Mesopotamia necessitated the establishment of garrisons and forts all along the desert frontier.[29] In Transjordan, forts were necessary because of the extension of the provincial boundaries of the province of Arabia to the north.[30] I aligned the frontier to the advantage of Arabia and detached parts of Syria-Phoenicia and added them to the province, which already included Petra, Jerash, Bosra and Legia. The city of Canatha became Septimia Canatha and joined the cities of Nabataean culture and traditions which now formed the province of Arabia, for the provinec of Arabia, thus named by Trajan, replaced the Nabatean kingdom which he annexed. To mark the importance of the province, dates beginning from 'the era of Bosra'[31] were established. I do not claim that I was the first emperor to recognise the importance of the province which Trajan had established – Petra was called Hadriane after Hadrian and Bosra called Triane after Trajan – but I enlarged Arabia. I also introduced Arabs into the court at Rome and thus allowed them for the first time to reach the pinnacle of Roman government. The Arabs like the · Carthaginians had been the victims of slander by Roman writers from Cicero on.[32] The eastern frontier was of more importance to me than to any other Roman ruler. The desert

Arabs, particularly the Palmyrenes, profited greatly from my policy of protecting the interior route through the desert of the Arabian peninsula.

I left, as part of the garrison on the Arabian frontiers, a contingent of Goths which I had used in the second Mesopotamian campaign.[33] For I followed the policy of keeping troops acquired by military victory far away from their own country. The experience I gained of protecting desert zones in Arabia helped me create similar outposts in Africa manned by Syrian troops.[34]

I started talking about Julia but instead I am thinking of Syria and Arabia, for to me she typified these two areas, so dear to my heart; which may explain why I married her. Was it the attraction of ancient roots, a nostalgia derived from racial memories, legends and tales? Or was it the memory of a summer night under the pale light of an eastern moon, with a delirious crowd on the temple esplanade of Emesa celebrating the marriage of the sun to earthly spouses, and the music accelerating to a frenzy of adoration and sexual ecstacy?[35] I remember, at the end of the festival, one of the tribunes who had accompanied me from Antioch where I was legate of the VI Scythia, pointed out to me the daughters of the Grand Priest. There was a hush among the crowd who were whispering, 'Julia Mamaea, Julia Domna,' while they made way for these two with their transparent veils and flashing jewels. One of the daughters tripped while passing and her veil was thrown back. They helped her back on her feet and, as she turned her face I glimpsed her. 'Julia Domna, Julia, Julia,' the crowd murmured. I retain the memory of her jet-black shiny hair, mixed with the myriad colours, the incense, the rhythmic dance; a frenzy of sensuality. It was a memory which returned to me, when, on the death of Marcia, I was in need of a bride. As my family was only equestrian and not very rich, I decided I should marry a princess, and a rich one at that! Marrying Julia was a predestined act, for she helped me towards that goal which I believed to be my fate – the throne. Her dynastic ambitions far exceeded mine. Later in our marriage she complained that I denied her the use of her brains and stemmed the flow of her energy, and the recriminations always ended by blaming Plautianus. How they made my life difficult those two, each pulling me this way and that. But it was a contest that Plautianus won.

It took Julia but a short time to realise that I no longer loved her. Her pride forbade her to believe that I was indifferent to her charms. Sometimes she reminded me how affectionate I had been in our first two years of marriage and her conclusion was: 'this was before Plautianus entered our lives.' My reply was, 'Plautianus has always been part of my life, although he is much younger than I; he is my kinsman and a Fulvi from my mother's family. We were inseparable in Leptis.' He re-entered my life after I marched on Rome and was of vital assistance to me. But how he hated Julia! The first time he set eyes upon her he said to me, unabashed, 'Septimius, how could a man like you succumb to a temple prostitute?' He saw the black flash in my eyes and cringed, for those words would have cost any other man his head, but I was overwhelmed with the joy of having him to myself once again. He was the pivot, the axis of my life. His cruel words about Julia shook me, but then I remembered the sexual frenzy around the temple in Emesa, and the details my soldiers told me of the orgies that followed the festivals. Could it be that the young Grand Priest's daughter was not immune to such a climate, where a kind of prostitution was sacred and where sex was so mixed up with religion?

Julia lived in great unhappiness[36], for I gave to Plautianus what she rightly thought was hers – love and attention – and a full share in the government, for I made him the praetorian prefect and shared with him my thoughts, my decisions and my acts. I hardly saw her, and she used to send her maid to the chamberlain to request an audience with the emperor. Her sarcasm, irony and Syrian wiles were wasted on me, and I used to play her game by granting her a formal audience.

65

I remember one occasion, when she came, haughty as ever, and found Plautianus with me. She ignored his presence and told me in a controlled voice that a wife had a right to talk to her husband privately, without vulgar outsiders. Before I could reply, Plautianus said, 'Dutiful and virtuous wives can!' I cut him short and Julia looked straight at me with blazing eyes. 'Does this man, whose antecedents all Rome knows, realise that he is talking in the presence of a Roman empress and a royal Arab princess?' Plautianus was stung, for he was known to have had a criminal past in Africa and he bowed mockingly. 'I know that the conduct of this empress does not entitle her to be Caesar's wife!' Julia walked out before I could stop her. I turned to Plautianus and told him that his manner towards Julia was outrageous[37], but instead of apologising, he told me that I was obstructing him from doing his duty towards me. Hadn't I appointed him praetorian prefect? Didn't I insist on upholding the morality laws? Didn't I believe that his first duty was to guard the imperial family from slander? Didn't I realise that rumours all over Rome spoke of Julia's adulterous conduct and that such rumours forced him to investigate?

I was boiling with rage and told him to come to the point. He pulled out a report and said, 'Here you will find evidence extracted from the women of the nobility.'[38] He was pale and his hands were trembling. He knew he had overplayed his hand. Enraged, I told him that he had committed a very grave error by conducting an investigation into my wife's conduct without my permission and that, knowing him, was sure he had extracted evidence from the noblewomen by torture.[39]

Plautianus answered in a cold, bitter tone, 'Is this the reward for my fidelity? Your wife is notorious for her adulteries[40] and you have only to look at this list of her lovers; it is right here.' 'No, no!' I shouted and dismissed him like a slave.

The charges poisoned my mind and turned me

completely against her. For weeks I neither saw nor addressed one word to her. I was waiting for my anger to abate before I faced her with the accusations.

Meanwhile, Julia took refuge in the study of philosophy and passed her days in her wing of the palace with sophists and men of letters[41]. She turned to philosophers and artists for consolation after she lost all influence over me. She became a patron of every art and a friend of every man of genius. Knowing my interest in judicial work, she had the three greatest jurists of the age, Ulpian, Paul and Papinian, in her intimate circle, and to those three fine minds I owe a great deal. She replaced my company with that of poets like Oppian, who compared her to Aphrodite Ouranienne and Venus Astarte.[42] With calculation and foresight, Julia turned her exile and estrangement from me into a cerebral retreat with a brilliant circle of intellectuals from all over the empire

The writers she collected wrote in both Greek and Latin, and discussion encompassed mathematics, astronomy, medicine and jurisprudence. This application to letters and philosophy gave her a splendid reputation, and gradually I lost my resolve to confront her with the accusations. All over the empire people talked of her beauty, magnetism, the strength of her mind and the wisdom of her judgements. In truth, Julia's salon, glittering with eminent names, was a great asset to the imperial house and helped me in my judicial work after Plautianus' death. I appointed a legal expert from her circle to the praetorian prefecture, Messius Saturninus, an African who wrote my speeches on legal matters. A literary expert, the sophist Aelius Antipater, became *ab epistilis graecus*; another sophist, Hermocrates of Phocea, served on the judicial council.[43]

I allowed Julia all the liberty she wanted with her artists and poets while enjoying to the full the company of Plautianus, who grew bolder and bolder. I could refuse him nothing. He even dared to joke in front of me about Syrian women and Julia's ageing father dressed in women's clothing and dancing around a stone! He despised the petty Arab dynasties in Petra, Palmyra, Hatra, Emesa, Edessa and Aleppo. Sometimes I imagine what fun he would have had here with me in Britain at the expense of the barbaric Caledonian chiefs, but alas, this is his sixth year in the grave.

In public, Julia was more regal than ever; she knew all too well of what she was accused and she told her entourage that I was condemning her on trumped up charges and the machinations of Plautianus.[44] She never displayed publicly any rift between us, though she never deigned to come to me and declare her innocence as she would not stoop to Plautianus' level.

As time went by, my resolve to face Julia faded. As a magistrate, I had doubts about the charges levelled against her by a man who was her enemy. The accusation, if true, would have given me grounds for divorce, but I decided against any action[45] because there was the dynasty to consider and Julia's ambitions for her sons. Without her, the throne was vulnerable. She was the intellectual face of power, and even though I had denied her a share in government, her influence was immense. I never fogot that she had helped me to legitimise the succession. It was on her advice that the coins and inscriptions of myself as an Antonine were first issued in Syria.[46] It was Julia and the army that pressured me to rename my seven-year-old son Bassianus, Marcus Antoninus, and to give him the title of Caesar. This had not been my plan, for I had intended that Albinus should succeed me. The break with him brought dire consequences: so many Romans dead, and an heir to the throne, a co-emperor, who was violent, irrational, and worse, still under Julia's constant control. I named my other son co-emperor just before the British Campaign. Julia was blind to the way her sons behaved in Rome, embezzling money and abusing boys. Their companions were gladiators and charioteers. It was Plautianus alone who controlled their conduct.

Under that cool façade Julia was boiling and plotting. She requested to see me one day and said, 'I have not come for myself, but for our son. All Rome knows that Plautianus has poisoned you against me so that he will succeed you.[47] He already behaves like an emperor, while you behave like his prefect. But now I hear that he has persuaded you to accept his ill-bred, adulterous, vulgar daughter as a wife for our son.[48] He has succeeded in keeping me away from you so that I cannot defend my son's interests, but you are deaf and blind. Have you not heard of the boys and girls Plautianus abuses?[49] Have you not heard of the hundred mature Roman men he castrated to keep as attendants for his daughter?[50] He has turned you, a sane man, into a besotted fool, but I say good luck to you when you take him into your bed after he has gorged himself and vomited![51] The degradation you descend to with him, however, is your affair. But I warn you, we are not going to throw our son into this cesspit with Plautianus and his daughter.'

Before I could open my mouth she walked out. I had never known her talk that way to me before, but I should have known that Julia would not take her humiliation lying down, and that under the cover of her sophisticated circle she was plotting revenge.

FOURTH NIGHT

The Talking Towers
of Byzantium

Eboracum (York)
1 February AD *211*

D id you know that walls can talk? I didn't, but the seven towers of Byzantium evidently spoke! I have this on the authority of no lesser person than the Senator Dio Cassius, who wrote a book on the omens and dreams that led me to the throne.[1]

The senator came to see me in AD 193, in the short period of thirty days that I spent in Rome during which I was declared emperor by the senate. I was preparing to leave for the east: I was in a hurry to move to the province of Asia to forestall Niger before he could occupy Byzantium and block my way to Syria. It was imperative for me to control the province that lay between us.

I questioned Dio on the area, for he is a native of the city of Nicea in Bithynia and knew Byzantium from his childhood. I told Dio that I shared his love of Byzantium, a fascinating city through which I had passed on many occasions, and I steered my questions towards its famous walls. It was then that he told me about the seven talking towers. Had it been anyone but the senator, I would have laughed at his telling me old wives' tales, but Dio is known for his integrity and erudition, and he claimed that he himself had heard them talk! He described the seven towers as extending from the Thracian gates to the sea and, according to him, if you threw a stone against the first tower, it not only echoed and 'spoke' itself, but also caused the second to do the same, and so on through the whole seven. Each received the sound from the one before, took the echo and sent it on.[2] Such wonders can only occur in Byzantium, the proud city, the most beautiful I have ever seen, including Rome, Antioch and Alexandria. They are majestic cities and each has its own distinctive elegance, but Byzantium's location and its monuments, raised as if by unseen powers, makes it a fitting dwelling not for men but for the gods; the city that I fell in love with each time I passed through and yet destroyed and reduced to ashes. Why am I destined to destroy what I love? All because of my pride. I could not forgive its stubborn resistance to my armies nor prevent it being a haven for Niger's renegade generals who took refuge within its walls. How did it withstand siege for so long, and what were the events that led to its destruction?

I do not blame Niger. The empire was a prize to be contended for and he and I, both proclaimed emperors, each tried to secure the province of Asia, especially Byzantium the bridge between two continents. I ordered the legions in Moesia to march into Thrace while I took the northern route along the Danube to mobilise troops for the campaign. Meanwhile, the governor of Asia, Asellius Aemilianus, already occupied Byzantines for Niger, hoping to block my passage over to Asia.[3] The governor of Thrace, Claudius Paterculienus, helped Niger because he bore a grudge against me for expelling him from the senate.[4]

Niger thus had the city, the largest and most prosperous in Thrace, for it benefited from shipping dues and fishing. I had to be content with neighbouring Perinthus, a rival of Byzantium, which my general Fabius Cilo captured with a Pannonian detachment.[5] The Byzantines felt secure within their enormous walls, constructed of massive squared stones fastened together by bronze plates, which held against my besieging armies. The seven talking towers were part of the walls, built at short intervals and not in a straight line, but rather a crooked circuit. The sections of the city wall on the land side were higher than where they faced the sea, for there the dangerous waters of the Bosphorus were an effective ally for the Byzantines who closed the harbours within the walls with chains.[6] And they had engines along the entire length of the wall; some hurled rocks and wooden beams and others had hooks which they let down suddenly to draw up our ships and siege engines.[7]

My army besieged them for three years with no result. The Byzantines even captured some of our ships. This they accomplished by sending divers to cut ships' cables under water and then drive nails into the hulls to which were attached ropes leading to the shore, so that the captured ships appeared to be moving of their own accord.[8] They built and repaired boats from timber taken from houses. They demolished the theatres and public monuments by taking the huge stones, bronze statues and other ornaments, and these they hurled on the besieging army. When all the supplies in the city had been consumed, the population was reduced to soaking hides and eating them.[9] To relieve the situation, they waited for rough weather and under cover of the storm and darkness, secured provisions from neighbouring villages, plundered the countryside for anything that could be called food. In their last extremity, they even devoured one another.[10]

Some of the population fled in boats during another storm, but my besieging army fell upon the craft and destroyed them. They were helpless as their boats were sunk and their belongings scattered over the water. The people watching the scene from the walls kept calling on the gods for help, but Zeus and Poseidon were deaf to the prayers, and when the desperate multitude saw their friends perishing in their boats, they sent up a chorus of groans and lamentations. They mourned for the rest of the day and the whole night. The next day, when the waves had subsided, the whole sea was red with blood and thick with corpses and wrecks.[11]

Byzantium and its population had touched the bottom of the abyss: all the former splendour had vanished, every material resource had been consumed and the last ounce of human strength was gone. There was no help from without, and the starved city was forced to surrender. The news reached me in far away Mesopotamia. The remnants of its people were without baths and theatres and all the former splendour had vanished.[12] Magistrates and soldiers were put to death. I confiscated the property of its citizens. I deprived Byzantium of its independence and granted the city and its territory to its hated rival, Perinthus.[13] The Perinthians treated it like a village and every day heaped insults on the Byzantines.

Unfortunately, my legates went beyond my orders in the destruction of the city. I was aghast when I heard of the extent of the devastation, for no one knew as well as I the military importance of this Roman outpost and base of operations against the barbarians of Pontus and Asia, and I hastened to make amends by ordering its restoration. The same old pattern: destruction and reconstruction! I rebuilt the walls, and in the centre of the city north of the great hippodrome I constructed a magnificent tetrastoon (place of the four porticoes). The decoration, I believe, has yet to be completed.[14] I refortified the Acropolis where the chief temples lay and repaired the theatre and amphitheatre on the side of the hill close to the shore. In the north, the stadium and strategion (headquarters) did not need much repair, but I spared no expense and the city began gradually to take on its splendid aspect again.

The destruction of Byzantium and the futile suffering of its people was the essence of Greek tragedy, for Byzantium was a Hellenic city, carrying in its bosom all the glory and weakness of ancient Greece. They joined the cause of Niger when he was alive and their loyalty survived his death, even though I sent his severed head to be shown along the walls to make them see they were fighting a lost cause. But it had no effect, because Byzantium was not fighting for Niger nor struggling desperately against me; they didn't really care which Roman emperor gained the throne. They were

Hellenes fighting their Roman conquerors.

Their holding of the city had given them an illusion of independence and freedom; for the space of three years Byzantium was a city state fighting a mighty empire. The legions within the city had a sprinkling of Romans, but most were Greeks recruited from Asia and Thrace and were fighting on Greek soil. My joy at hearing of the surrender turned to grief when I heard the gruesome details. I mourned the beautiful city and bowed my head for its agony, and in a split second of time I saw the ominous cycles of fate hanging over the city which in generations to come, would repeat the same illusions, the same despair. Could it be that certain places, by their locations or perhaps by ancient maledictions, invite recurrent tragedies? The fall of Byzantium led my reflections far and wide. It seemed to me that Niger and I, by an accident of fate fighting for the Roman empire in its Greek provinces, were really fighting the wars between the Greek cities. Our civil war was the catalyst that brought back this legacy of ancient rivalry[15], a long-standing weakness of the Greeks. It was, this mutually destructive tendency that had led to Macedonian domination and Roman conquest. It was this rivalry that had led Perinthus to support me when Byzantium was held by Niger, and it was because Nicomedia in Bithynia welcomed my army and offered full co-operation that the important city of Nicea, only thirty miles away, opened its gates to Niger's army and took any fugitive that came its way. The two cities became rival camps and bases from which the two forces clashed.[16]

If I partially understood the rivalry between the Greek cities of Thrace and Bithynia, I could not comprehend at all how this malady existed in cities in Syria with a Canaanite-Phoenician indigenous population and only a sprinkling of Greek settlers and Roman officials where, although the official language was Greek, the natives spoke Aramaic. I was wrong in thinking that these cities had only acquired a Hellenistic façade five centuries ago. The truth is that

Hellenism had penetrated with all its virtues and defects and they had become more Greek than the Greeks!

Upon the return of Niger to Antioch after his defeat at Cyzicus Laodicea declared for me against Antioch. These two cities had been founded by the Seleucids and are only fifty miles apart.[17] Strife also broke out in two Canaanite-Phoenician cities: Tyre, the mother city of the western Phoenicians, and Berytus, a coastal town. Tyre declared for me against Berytus. On hearing of the rebellion of Loedicia and Tyre Niger was so angered that he dispatched some Moroccan spearmen and a detachment of archers with orders to kill the citizens, seize the movable property in the cities and to burn buildings. The fierce Moroccans fell upon Laodicea and then turned to Tyre where they looted, killed, burned and destroyed.[18]

The fate of Niger haunts me, for I know now through what dejection and despair he passed. His forces were proving superior on the field of Issus – where previously Darius had fought and lost to Alexander – and he was full of hope until heaven turned against him in the form of a thunderstorm. This sign from the gods inspired my troops, and Niger's fleeing forces perished by the thousand.[19] The loss of life was so great that the rivers of the plain carried more blood than water down to the sea.[20] After this decisive defeat, Niger, riding a fast horse, escaped with a few of his men to Antioch. There he found the population evacuating the city and the place full of weeping and lamentation as the people mourned their brothers and sons fallen in battle. Alas for Antioch that their youth, though enthusiastic and willing to face any danger for Niger's sake, was untried in battle and had none of the endurance, experience and quality of my own Illyrian troops.[21]

So, a lonely man who had lost all hope, Niger rode out of Antioch to the suburbs, but my pursuing cavalry caught up with him and beheaded him. Merciless fate made him pay the price for his mistakes; but did my scheming seal his fate? Do I really want to give an account of what I believe to be the reasons for his defeat, reasons historians of the civil wars made little of? Niger's failure is attributed by them to his lack of intelligence[22]; and yet he had so many advantages over me. He was an Italian, loved by the Roman *plebs*, and he was governor of Syria, from a military point of view one of the most important posts of the empire. He was vain and loved it when his entourage called him the new Alexander.[23] His vanity also manifested itself in overconfidence. Take the coins he issued as emperor in Antioch – his portrait was ugly, accentuating his long narrow head, thick lips and tense expression.[24] I knew him to be much better looking than that. I, on the other hand, made my portraits more flattering! In fact, I insisted on many samples from different artists and then chose the most flattering, as did Julia) Niger didn't know how to win over the public or make use of legends on his coins. He was as Commodus described him, negative. But above all, he did not believe in his destiny, for he could have defeated me at Perinthus when he by advancing from his headquarters in Byzantium, allowed unfavourable omens to dissuade him: an eagle reportedly perched upon a military standard and remained there until it was captured and bees made a honeycomb around Niger's image! For these reasons he returned to Byzantium.[25]

All these elements contributed to his defeat but they were not the determining factors. The truth is that Niger was vanquished not because I was abler or more decisive but because I kidnapped his children. To that alone I attribute his defeat. I did not invent the practice of seizing children as hostages; Commodus held the children of provincial governors as guarantees of their loyal support. Knowing this, when I was declared emperor by my soldiers, I secretly smuggled my children out of Rome to prevent them falling into the hands of a rival[26], and, as soon as I arrived in Rome, I sent Plautianus on a secret mission to seize the children of Niger and all the children of the governors of the east.[27]

The pro-Consul of Asia, Asellius, a man of

SEPTIMIUS SEVERUS – COUNTDOWN TO DEATH

understanding and experience and governor of Syria before Niger[28], remained neutral at the start of hostilities so, to be on the safe side, I kidnapped his children also. This was not a wise precaution, for eventually, despite my sequestering of his children, he joined Niger and I was afraid that as a relative of Albinus, he would try to achieve a rapprochement between Albinus and Niger behind my back. Niger named Asellius commander and, as I said, he seized Byzantium for him.

The children were kept in custody at court, serving a dual purpose: governors might, in their anxiety for their offspring, betray Niger's cause, or, if they remained loyal to him, I had the means to harm them before they harmed me.

The method worked, for Asellius Aemelianus, the commander of Niger's forces, eventually betrayed him. Some claim that he betrayed Niger out of jealousy, since he had had the more distinguished career and could not stomach the idea of Niger as his superior and emperor.[29] The defeat and retreat of both men before Perinthus was, I am sure, partly due to their deep concern for their children who were in my hands. Hoping to save his children, Niger sent me a proposal for joint rule, but I rejected it with scorn, replying instead that I would promise him an undisturbed exile if he wished it, but that I refused to pardon Asellius[30] and would ask the Senate to declare them both enemies of the State.[31]

This reply made them desperate. Asellius, with a large force, was defeated at the Hellespont, near Perninthus – for just before the battle he received a letter from his children, begging him to consider their safety.[32] (Needless to say, I dictated the letter!) Asellius lost heart, and in defeat he fled with a number of generals. But he was pursued and slain near Cyzicus. Niger's heart was not in the battles that followed, and, true to character, he lost them all.

I risk boring future young Romans by writing about my hollow victory over Niger and boasting of his failure. What

irony that for me, man of many failures, the memory of
Hatra, the city of Shemesch, should rankle for the last
thirteen years!

True failure attracts more attention than success. To
think that my failure to subdue Hatra – a small fortress in
the middle of nowhere, desolate and lost in the desert –
remained a more powerful memory than the conquest and
sack of Ctesiphon, fabulous capital of the Parthian empire.
Perhaps I exaggerate. It may be that my memory is playing
games with the sequence of time by emphasising things the
world considers trivial and glossing over events considered
important – if true, this memoir would seem to be only an
absurd smokescreen to hide the truth. But I give my memory
free rein. For example, my mind passes lightly over the
battle of Issus in Cilicia, my triumph against Niger with
20,000 of his soldiers slain, and barely remembers the other
battles against him near Cyzicus on the Hellespont and at
Nicea. But it persists in brooding over Byzantium which
Niger's army held against me for three long years. As to my
struggle against Albinus, my memory absolutely refuses to
recall the scene of horror near Lyon when I nearly lost the
battle and came very close to calamity and it assiduously
shuns the civil wars in general because they were anathema
to me; a time when Roman killed Roman.

But Hatra remains clear in my mind. Three years after I
abandoned the siege I was back in Rome. There, I found
work was continuing on the triumphal arch decreed by the
Senate after my first Parthian campaign in AD 195. The arch
is located in the forum, and the idea was to make the battle
scenes so realistic, portrayed like an open book, that if you
looked up you relived the whole campaign. Masons,
sculptors, architects and artists laboured in the workshops
of Rome. Military experts ensured that tunics and arms,
ours and the enemy's, were correctly portrayed. There were
great rows whenever a sculptor depicted the wrong hat on a
captive or the wrong turning of a military chariot. I often
went to watch the work, and was often consulted lest any

detail was forgotten.

One day I was told that the official in charge of the project requested an audience. 'Caesar,' said he, very embarrassed, 'we have reached the last battle of the campaign, that of Hatra, and the military historian attached to the Parthian expedition has given me a detailed account of it.' I raised my hand to cut him short because I knew what he wanted to ask. How should the artists depict my defeat before the walls of Hatra?

'I should have thought of that,' I said, 'for you cannot show defeat on an arch of triumph, nor expose to the public and posterity the retreat of the mighty Roman army before a minor Arab chief at the walls of the city of Shemesh.'

'But Caesar,' he said humbly, 'you have had many victories: we have carved in brilliant relief the siege and capture of Nisibis, Seleucia, Babylon and Ctesiphon.'

'True.' I answered. 'But this poses a dilemma. In principle, no manipulation of the truth should be attempted to hide our defeat. On the other hand, can you imagine veterans returning to Rome and seeing a fictitious scene of victory at Hatra on the arch? I shudder to think of their reaction. But the official position is that Hatra is a vassal of Parthia and thus can be considered defeated as its overlord has been defeated.[33] It therefore can be omitted from the historical record. My instruction is that you deal with the question on that basis.'

In speaking of Hatra, I first have to summarise through the two Parthian campaigns which preceded it. On my arrival in Syria I had planned to attack Hatra first, for I had learned that its king Barsemius had supplied a force of archers to my enemy Niger. Looking back, I wonder why I embarked on a policy of conquest and annexation following in the path of Trajan and not in the footsteps of Hadrian, who made peace and renounced the conquests of Trajan. But, the gods know, I had at the time plenty of reasons for such a belligerent policy. In the aftermath of the civil war, a foreign adventure was required to unite the recently-warring legions against a common enemy. I also needed to prove my military power and to recover the Roman soldiers, skilled engineers and mechanics who had fled to Parthia after the defeat of Niger and who had failed to return after I declared an amnesty. They were now teaching the enemy our military tactics and showing them how to manufacture arms to fight us.

The Parthians gave me the excuse, for they incited their vassals, the Osrhoeni, Adiabeni and Mesopotamian Arabs, to shake off the control the Romans had exercised over them since the expedition of Lucius Verus; but they should have known better than to try to enlarge their territories at our expense! The tribes seized Nisibis, a Roman outpost. When I heard of this, I crossed the Euphrates into enemy territory with a large force and, in spite of the heat and dust storms, relieved Nisibis.[34] I sent my generals into the surrounding areas to capture the cities and lay waste to the land. King Abgar of the Osrhoene was allowed to retain his capital Edessa and limited territory surrounding it; the dynasty of Abgar resembles that of Emesa, as they too were bedouins from the desert who had adopted the use of Aramaic,[35] but I punished the Osrhoeni for their defection, making their kingdom a Roman province with a procurator, and I overran the territory of the Scenite Mesopotamian Arabs. The Parthian vassal kingdom of Adiabene east of the Tigris acknowledged Roman sovereignty.[36] I fortified Nisibis as a bulwark of Syria and bestowed upon myself the titles, Parthicus Arabicus and Parthicus Adiabenicus. Later I dropped the Parthicus out of consideration for the Parthians' feelings.

A coin was minted to commemorate the campaign showing Arab and Adiabeni captives sitting back to back on a round shield with their hats on[37]. I keep the coin with me as a talisman, my first triumph against the enemy. This triumph prompted me to consider conquering Parthia itself but my plans for an extensive campaign were interrupted by the news that Albinus had declared himself emperor and was crossing the Channel with his three British legions into Gaul, possibly on his way to Rome. This meant another civil war. I consulted the army who declared him a public enemy, and I made preparations for the march to Gaul. But before I left I established a new province of Mesopotamia with Nisibis as its capital garrisoned with two legions – I and II Parthica.

I was disturbed by the news that the people of Rome, on hearing rumours of the impending civil war, had assembled in the circus to demonstrate against this new development. For there was no room for two emperors and I believed that Albinus had no chance of winning this war. The governor of Lyon refused to recognise him but he did have the support of the governor of Spain. My main worry was the senate in which his supporters were in a majority; and although we were both Africans, he had the advantage of having been born in the senatorial rank. I ordered the closing of the Alpine passes and decided to leave the army at Poetovo and go to Rome. In Rome, I obtained from the senate a declaration naming Albinus as public enemy, and to placate the populace I held games and gave donations. I left for Gaul through Noricum along the road I had repaired only a year previously. Albinus was defeated at the battle of Lyon, and the town was sacked and burned. I had his head sent to the senate before my arrival, as a warning. In Rome, I executed twenty-nine senators who had supported Albinus and confiscated their estates. The income from these estates went into a new exchequer – *res privata* which was at my personal disposal.

During my absence from the east Volgases, the Parthian king, overran the new province of Mesopotamia and laid siege to Nisibis. Returning from Rome I immediately crossed the Euphrates and ordered boats to be constructed of timber from the abundant forests along the river. The Parthians did not wait for my arrival but lifted the siege of Nisibis and retreated homewards. I seized Seleucia which had been in ruins since it was sacked by the Roman general

Cassius thirty years before; I captured Babylon – deserted by the Parthians – but soon abandoned it myself. The Parthian capital Ctesiphon fell after only token resistance but Volgases escaped with some cavalry. I let him get away into the interior of Parthia but I secured the royal treasury with all his jewels. I took 10,000 captives who were later sold in the slave markets of Rome, and I allowed my troops – exhausted and racked with disease – to plunder the town.[38] The Senate conferred on me the title Parthicus Maximus, first given to Trajan, and offered me a triumph, but I declined because of gout (I was unable to stand in a chariot).[39] My sons had already received the titles of Augustus and Caesar.[40] I returned by a different route because the army had exhausted all the provisions on the outward march and we were obliged to feed on the roots of plants. Part of the army went by land, the other by boats on the Tigris.

My enemies in Rome – and they were legion – criticised my campaign, calling it a raid and attributing it to vainglory rather than any real need to guard the frontiers. The Parthian war gave me the legitimacy I needed, especially with the added territories, but I now realise the burden that these territories have been on the empire, draining funds from the treasury and posing the constant threat of frontier wars.[41] Maybe I have repeated the same mistakes here in Britain, embarking on an all-out subjugation of the island – which brings with it the threat of future rebellions – and squandering our resources. I have already received reports from the treasury that Britain already costs Rome more than it brings in.[42]

But to return to the east in AD 198, there was Hatra, the sacred city, awaiting me in the desert. Hatra! What feelings that word evokes! I feel the dryness of the desert in my throat, even here in the British damp, and the relentless glare of the sun burning my eyes. My feet throb as I stand watching the battle. It was there I believe that my fatal illness began.

The strategists pointed out that Hatra had to be taken as it was the only stronghold remaining between the Tigris and Euphrates and the provinces of Mesopotamia and Syria which was not under direct Roman rule. Its importance to Rome was not only military but economic, for it was the centre of the caravan trade between east and west. The reports of my scouts described it as being at the top of a precipitous ridge, encircled by enormously strong walls over a mile in diameter.[43] The city is circular with a sacred enclosure in the middle grouping together the many sanctuaries. The entrance gate to the sacred precinct has three doors and four towers resembling a Roman triumphal arch. The enclosure itself has several inner courts and an esplanade for pilgrims. Next to the entrance is the Hellenistic temple of the sun god Maran, the most ancient in the city. The rest of the temples are a series of vaulted Iwans (large halls), of which the most important is the southern one which takes the form of cube with an altar to Maran surrounded by a vaulted corridor for the liturgical circumambulation. An inscription on the door requests worshippers to enter with bare feet and casts a malediction upon those who enter otherwise.[44] This is the famous temple of fire consecrated to the sun where the ritual plays on the duality of light and shadow. Stairs through the thick wall lead up to the roof where the burning of incense is conducted in the open air.

The northern Iwan has an altar to the moon goddess Martan, spouse of Maran, who has the traits of Aphrodite-Venus. The trinity at the summit of the Hatran religious pantheon consists of Maran, Martan and their son Bir-Maran who has the attributes of Apollo, Dionysus and Mithra.[45] Other Iwans have stone seats built along the walls for the sacred banquets like those in Petra and Palmyra where the different tribes participate in a common cult to the memory of the dead. The wine, bread and meat of the sacrificed animals provides an association between men and gods. Hellenistic, Parthian, Aramaean and Arab gods co-exist in the Hatran pantheon and the Arab goddess Allat is represented in the form of Athena.

The cult of death is very important in their religion and Hatra, like Petra, has tombs everywhere. To me the most interesting cult is the worship of Hercules which they borrowed from Syria; they consider him the protector of their kings, a strange coincidence as Hercules is one of the titular gods of my house! The kings of Hatra, the historians tell me, were tribal chiefs, high priests and leaders of the army. They called themselves kings of the Arabs for the population is Arab, but Aramaic is the official language. The desert caravans enriched them and allowed them to build sumptuous sanctuaries and numerous palaces. The city is well defended by a double stone wall.

The scant knowledge I received from agents and historians only made me thirst for more. I wanted to know all about this sacred mysterious city which had been a legend to the Romans since Trajan, for he had failed to conquer it. I had a yearning to enter the temple of fire and to offer on its roof a sacrifice to the sun. However, my actual knowledge of Hatra came from a bedouin named Aziz, a desert guide employed by the army during our march to Nisibis, my first campaign against the Parthian enemy.

On crossing the Euphrates into enemy territory we seemed lost in a desolate land with no water and not a single blade of grass. I called the guide and berated him. 'Where is the water you promised, Aziz? And where are these hidden pools that you alone know of?' Suddenly a dust storm rose from nowhere and caused such havoc that the soldiers could neither march nor even talk. I turned to Aziz, clutched him by the neck and nearly strangled him. 'Liar, impostor! Where is the spring you promised?'

'It is near, a few steps Caesar. Just walk on a little more, I beg you.' We struggled through the dust until he brought us to a stagnant pool in the sand. It was black and green with filth, fungus and creeping creatures. The soldiers ran toward, then stopped disgusted, and although dying of thirst, would not go near or touch the water. I called for a cup, filled it with the repugnant muddy syrup and drained it in view of them all. Others followed, drank and were refreshed.[46] When night fell and my conference with my officers and scouts to plan the next day's march was over, I was lying by the camp fire, for desert nights are icy cold. Aziz crept up beside me without ceremony, for an emperor was nothing to him – he was equal to any man – and said, 'Caesar, you are fit to be a great tribal chief!'I laughed and told him that calling an emperor a tribal chief was no compliment. 'To us, great Caesar,' he said, 'a tribal chief acts as the servant of the whole tribe. That is why he is selected a chief, and today you acted like one. Listen to what our poet says.

> 'If you reproach your friend for every fault,
> Friends, one by one, will leave you behind.
> If you don't deign to drink with dirt and mud
> You have great thirst
> For who can always clear water find?'

I kept Aziz through the night while he told me tales of Nisibis our next stop, of the Chaldeans and of the magicians and ghosts of Babylon and Seleucia. One Greek ghost in Babylon screeched every evening, 'Alexander, Alexander, why did you leave us here?'

'And strangest of all...' began Aziz. Then, having second thoughts, he said, 'Caesar, have you ever heard that spectres and ghosts have filthy tongues? People who understand the Greek language say they heap curses and maledictions on their ancient kings – Antiochus, Seleucius and even on Iskander of the horns – but I cannot repeat the worst words, just, 'May you dwell in Hades, may you remain in the underworld forever!''

Aziz spoke of Hatra, the mysterious city of Shemesh, of its temples which he described minutely, of its treasures that came as gifts to the sun from all over the earth. I questioned him about the sanctuaries, and he spoke of the temple of fire and how the priest magicians played light against dark and how incense formed thick clouds over the roof which went straight to heaven, and of the delicious drowsiness it caused amongst the worshippers. He spoke of the Hatran women with their lofty headdresses and their veils, and said they all looked like queens, sparkling with precious stones and trailing their Parthian silk robes with folds falling to the ground. He did not understand their religion, nor did he wish to, but he admitted he was attracted to their worship of Samya; the military standards, with their special temple and priests. He described a funerary feast he had once attended, with priests, soldiers and common people seated on couches in a dining room which was cool even at high noon. I urged him to tell me more night after night throughout our march. In a whisper, glancing over his shoulder, he spoke of the wealth that built the temples and palaces in the midst of nowhere. "It must have been spirits (*djinn*) who built the colossal monuments for no man can build such splendour in the desert!' His tales were music to my ears and only strengthened my desire to occupy Hatra one day.

On our last night near the walls of Nisibis I asked Aziz if he wished to join our army as an irregular soldier with good pay. He looked at me for the first time with disdain and said with a contempt he could not disguise, 'Caesar, do you want to put me in chains? Do you want me to leave all this?' His hand swept the empty land and the stars. 'I cannot sleep under a roof, nor can I follow your childish games!" I suppose he meant our daily drills and military exercises. And then he went on dreamily, "Caesar, my home is the desert with its silence, its sudden winds, its perfume. Do you smell the perfume, Caesar?"

'No, Aziz,' I replied, perplexed.

'The desert perfume, Caesar, is the lack of smell, and its music is silence, not the cacophony of noises that city dwellers love.' I was very moved but kept silent so as not to break the spell he had woven. I wanted to tell him that I too loved the empty space and the stars and I wanted to enter Hatra, not as a conqueror, but as a humble devotee of the sun.

It was to be three years from that night before I could turn my attention to Hatra. I first investigated the reasons for the Trajan's failure and then prepared for the siege. I was driven by my passion and longing for the city. My siege engineers had to take account of the outer stone wall, three metres thick, and its 163 towers. Reports gave me detailed plans of gateways and what were considered to be weak points in the walls. I started the attack with every kind of siege engine and left no technique untried, but I accomplished nothing.

So many soldiers perished or were wounded I feared my army would be annihilated.[47] The only siege engines that were not destroyed were those designed by a Greek named Priscus who had built engines for the defence of Byzantium against me. Learning of his skill, I prevented his execution after the surrender of the city and had him build the machines for the siege of Hatra.[48] Like Trajan's soldiers before them, my troops could not stand the excessive heat. They fell ill and died and I lost men and money. The Hatrans hurled missiles from their walls and poured hot naphtha over my troops.[49] The Arab archers and their famous cavalry sneaked out of the gates and assailed us violently from behind.

Already deeply depressed I was infuriated when Plautianus and some of his associates insinuated that the reason for the bad performance of the army was the presence of subversive instigators in their midst. Playing on my weakness where divination is concerned, they affirmed that some of my legates had been consulting astrologers and asking Chaldeans and soothsayers how long I was destined to live. What irony, for Commodus accused me of the same crime in Sicily! They summoned a soldier named Valerius who had heard Julius Crispus the praetorian tribune quote

Virgil sarcastically, 'In order that Turnus may marry Livinia, we are meanwhile perishing unheeded.'[50] I interpreted this as a literary allusion to my delaying the assault for private reasons. I had the tribune executed on the spot and appointed the accuser in his place, but my interpretation was wrong, for Julius Crispus was only expressing the mood of the whole army and its fury at the pointlessness of the siege.

My frustration grew. Plautianus pointed to Laetus who had become a thorn in my flesh. The soldiers loved him and hung on his every word; he was more popular than me! I was mad with jealousy, for these were the soldiers who had marched with me to Rome. The reputation of Laetus as a fine man, in private and public, in peace or war, made it worse. My suspicion of him rested on the fact that he seemed qualified for imperial power but I hesitated for he was a former legate and held Nisibis for me against the enemy. Above all, he was the general who had saved me from defeat against Albinus near Lyon, but there was no denying that he was too popular with the troops. Plautianus convinced me of the threat Laetus posed to me. I nodded my head in assent, and he was executed.[51] I immediately ordered a general assault before the soldiers heard of the execution, and soon I could see my troops about to force their way through a breach in the wall[52] and enter the city.

I still cannot explain what happened to me then. I was in a trance, images passed before my eyes. I saw soldiers plundering the temple treasures and offerings, vast sums of money accumulated from humble worshippers over many years. They would surely claim the right to plunder after the hardships, the disease and heat they had endured, and as they had come to expect plunder after Ctesiphon. I saw them wrecking and desecrating the sanctuaries, for they were angry, and nothing could appease them. Nor would I be able to stop them. Another image passed like a flash. I saw myself condemning these proud Arabian nobles and chiefs, knights and archers to captivity and chains. I could not endure the thought. It was like capturing beautiful wild animals for the arena. I felt very akin to the Hatrans and I could not humiliate such a proud race. I wanted them to come to terms, to surrender voluntarily, to avoid being captured and enslaved.[53] I remembered that Hercules, the protector of their kings, was the patron of my native city, Leptis. I later built a temple to Hercules in Rome, and ordered his statue to figure on the triumphal arch. All this passed before me in an instant of time and at that moment I did the unthinkable, the unpardonable: I sounded the trumpet for retreat! The army went mad! I had deprived them of their triumph and of the booty in Hatra, and by now they had heard about Laetus. I was faced with a mutiny. I disclaimed all responsibility for the death of Laetus and denied I had ever given the order. I put all the blame on those who had killed him.[54] I explained to the troops my reasons for sounding the retreat, but it was no use. I waited the whole of the next day for the Hatrans to seek peace but no one came; instead they worked all night to repair the section we had breached.[55] My despair and frustration knew no bounds. I decided to resume the assault, but the European soldiers were so angry they refused to obey. I compelled the Syrians to attack and they were utterly destroyed.[56] The brutes from Germany, Pannonia and the Danube had the ability to fight, for their blood was not diluted by past civilisations like the tired Greeks and Syrians. The contrast between the over-civilised Hellenistic east and the barbarians never ceased to amaze me. It is these northern brutes that constitute the future danger for Rome, and in moments of clarity I blame myself for being too absorbed with securing and expanding the eastern frontiers of the empire at the expense of the western borders, where the danger lies.

That was not the end of Hatra. The failure of the first siege did not destroy my ambitions. I obstinately started new and even more massive preparations for another attack, for I could not stomach the defiant resistance of the

Plate 1
Marble bust of Septimius Severus – portrait in the guise of Serapis.
(*Museo Capitolino, Rome*).

▲ *Plate 3*
Marble bust of Julia Domna, found in Castel Porziano in the vicinity of Rome, first decade of the 3rd century AD. *Glyptothek, Munich)*

◄ *Plate 2*
Septimius Severus. Marble bust from Leptis Magna (*Djemila Archaeological Museum, Algeria*).

Plate 4
Caracalla, on the ocasion of his becoming sole ruler, AD 211
(*Louvre, Paris*).

Plate 5
Geta as a boy, *c.* AD 200 (*Glyptothek, Munich*).

Plate 6
The Arch of Septimius Severus (Rome), AD 203:
Taking of Sleucia.

Plate 7
The Arch of Septimius Severus (Rome), AD 203:
Taking of Ctesiphon

Plate 9 (top)
Portrait of the Severan Family: Septimius Severus, Julia Domna, Caracalla and Geta (erased). Painted on wood from al-Fayum in Egypt *c.* AD 199.

Plate 8 (bottom)
Septimius Severus coin, AD 198-210.

Plate 10 Marble relief: Homage of the Senate to Septimius Severus (Rome), AD 205.

round fortress, holding out alone when all around was subdued. The second siege lasted twenty days[57] before I abandoned it and retired to review the situation prior to leaving for Egypt by way of Palestine.[58]

I moved my headquarters away from the walls of Hatra in order to be alone to review the factors which had led to the defeat. Primarily it was the refusal of the European soldiers, in particular the Pannonians, to return to the assault.[59] But it is to these same soldiers that I owe the throne. Hatra had taught me that power has limits and that sharing the army's hardships, eating their food and sleeping in their tents is not enough. A commander must be just and impartial. At Hatra, the soldiers doubted my integrity, whispering that I was an adept of Shemesh, that I had ordered the retreat because I was struck with awe before the Hatran sun god and that I had killed their beloved Laetus for no reason other than pure jealousy. As a magistrate and jurist I tried to analyse the army's case impartially.

The major accusation against me was that I pampered the troops and caused them to be insolent. I was accused of undermining the austerity of the soldiers' diet and lessening their respect for their commanders.[60] I was also accused of excessive generosity in increasing their pay from three hundred to five hundred denari. However, depreciation of the currency and the rise in prices fully justified the increase. The conservatives criticised what they called my bribery of the army because I would pay bonuses in gold to compensate for the deductions for rations and clothing. These critics pointed to increased civilian taxes[61] but these civilians could only carry on their professions and trades thanks to the soldiers securing the frontiers and keeping the peace. They thought I was teaching the soldiers to be greedy for riches and ease. They pointed to Europos, the farthest town on the frontier of Parthia, where I allowed soldiers to live in quarters in the town and to have clubs and entertainment.[62] They forgot how isolated and hard life is for the legions on the frontiers, living under constant threat from the enemy. I believe I was justified in trying to make life bearable for them. The greatest complaint against me was that I abolished the practice of selecting the praetorian guard exclusively from Italy, Spain, Macedonia and Noricum and opened recruitment to all legions alike. Membership became a kind of prize for bravery in battle or for soldierly conduct, but now I am blamed for ruining the youth of Italy. [63]

My opening up of the army to barbarians is a simple acceptance of the fact that the empire needs more men. Augustus fixed the number of legions at twenty-eight. Trajan had thirty legions, and I have raised three more. I have increased the numbers of auxiliaries, especially mounted archers from Osrhoene and Palmyra, and have dispatched them to all fronts. I have made recruitment almost wholly compulsory. [64]

To integrate soldiers in society I have not only raised their pay but allowed under-officers and centurions to wear gold rings, the mark of free birth, a concession which has brought them closer to equestrian rank. [65] I have given formal recognition to their union with native women or concubines; cohabitation was already widespread and soldiers used to have to wait for retirement from active service to be married. [66] To stabilise the security of our frontiers, I have granted frontier garrisons land allotments and have allowed them income from farming and workshop products in times of peace. [67] These settled military establishments on the frontier have increased the tempo of Romanisation. The sons of frontiersmen have remained in the army, and the dwellings on the frontier area have already become small villages.

I have given soldiers the right to form unions to protect the interests of their members. Above all, I have transformed the officer class allowing entry to men from the ranks who are of course of a lower social status. [68] The bulk of the army is recruited from peasants. I have improved the camps with stone walls, enclosed barracks, temples, colonnaded courtyards, store rooms and large bathrooms with central heating.[69]

All these measures had as their objective to make the service more attractive and profitable in order to keep the men loyal and to prevent desertion. A necessary objective, surely, in these changing times, for the territories I added beyond the Euphrates and the extension of the provinces of Syria and Arabia into the desert have altered the shape of the empire. I also moved frontiers forward in Africa, but I neglected the west until the British expedition. The empire needs more troops and I have been blamed for turning barbarians into soldiers for the empire, but the critics have forgotten the decline of our manpower reserves due to the freeing of slaves. The freeing of slaves came about partly as a result of the trend towards greater equality, which I encouraged. (New cults like Christianity were also preaching equality, but that in no way influenced my attitude.) The empire, to survive, has to adapt to changing circumstances and use the resources it can obtain.

My reflections have convinced me that whatever I have done to improve the soldier's lot has been rewarded by the devotion and loyalty of the army, and now, here in York, thirteen years after the incident in Hatra, I cannot praise the army highly enough. They have borne with fortitude extreme hardship. The security of the empire is in their hands and I am not ashamed to confess that they occupy a special place in my heart; whatever privileges or indulgences I have granted them are hardly adequate. In the camps they revere the emperor more than the standards, and I revere them more in return. My last thoughts are for them, and to my two co-emperor sons my dying words will be, 'Remain united, enrich the soldiers and despise all others.'[70]

FIFTH NIGHT

Egyptian Magic

Eboracum (York)
2 February AD *211*

Egypt has always fascinated me. Ever since my only visit eleven years ago I have been longing to return, for I have never enjoyed myself as I did on that trip.[1] I found it painful to tear myself away but I had been absent a year and a Roman Emperor must show himself sometimes in Rome. I passed through Palestine on my way and made Sebastia a *colonia*. I changed the name of the towns of Beit Jibrin to Eleutheropolis and Lydda to Diospolis, and permitted them to use my name on their coins.[2] The two towns took the year of my passage as the commencement of a new era and started to date from it.

Officials in Palestine complained to me about numerous conversions to Judaism and Christianity. I instructed them strictly to forbid this practice under threat of heavy penalties[3] and promised an edict to that effect on my return to Rome. I continued my journey by land and stopped at Pelusium where I sacrificed to the spirit of Pompey at the tomb which the emperor Hadrian had built on his visit to Egypt. My adopted father was a descendant of Pompey and I revered him as the general who conquered the east but found it repulsive that the renegade Roman murderer of Pompey had the same name as myself, 'Lucius Septimius'.[4]

My visit to Egypt was welcomed, as no emperor had visited Egypt since Hadrian sixty years previously.[5] I sailed up the Nile and visited the whole country but could not proceed beyond the frontier with Ethiopia because of pestilence.[6] I visited the Pyramids and the Sphinx and the colossal singing statue of Amenophis III in Thebes.[7] I ordered the repair of the crumbling statue, but I am told that after the repair it never again gave its sunrise song.[8]

At Philae (Aswan) I took over from the prefect the ceremony which the ancient Pharaohs, regarded as gods by the Egyptians, performed in May. The ceremony consisted of my throwing gold and silver into a rock cave by the sacred river Nile.[9] There I was, dressed in the garb of the Pharaohs (against the advice of my staff) standing on the garlanded royal boat, enveloped by the smoke of incense and perfumes, flowers and herbs. I was lulled by the hypnotic chants of the priests who stood on the banks of the river echoing each other with melodies that rose to a crescendo, and these were followed by a thousand trumpets which seemed to open heaven itself upon the glittering river. It was in that moment when I had to step forward to throw the gifts that I became Pharaoh. I was no longer Septimius Severus to the official who shaded me with an umbrella; I was the incarnation of the Pharaoh, the ruler of Upper and Lower Egypt. I was Ra, Osiris, Isis and Horus. A change came over my physical body. My stature seemed to stretch; my features shrank and my eyes became narrower, my chin lengthened and my hands developed thin tapering fingers as I started to throw the gold and silver into the cave. With the last throw, the changes in my body were reversed, and again I became Roman Emperor, ruler of Upper and Lower Egypt, with thirty-three legions at my command, a war machine that no Pharaoh had ever known.

That moment at Philae had far reaching effects, for when I came back to myself, the priests were bowing to the ground. Their eyes were lowered as if they were afraid to look upon my face, as if its brilliance would injure them, and I realised that they must have seen and felt my metamorphosis. The chief priest moved towards me, knelt to the ground and addressed me as a god. It was there and then that the Egyptians identified me with Serapis, and the tradition of my portraits in the guise of Serapis with the four corkscrew curls and forked beard was confirmed.[10] A portrait was painted in Egypt with Julia and my two sons[11], but I was a devotee of Serapis before I went to Egypt and my sculptured portrait as such appeared later on the arch of the Argentari.[12]

How time smoothes the edges. I am amused now at my fury when my enemies claimed that I chose Serapis as my tutelary divinity to associate myself with Commodus, my adopted brother in an attempt to legitimise my claim to the throne.[13] It was the Egyptians who made the identification and linked me with the ruler of the lower world, whilst I was in fact already associated with Jupiter, the ruler of the upper world – as the many reliefs (especially those in Leptis) show.[14]

But I must go back to that night at Philae, for after the exhilaration of the ceremony came utter exhaustion, and I made it known to the Egyptians that my attending a banquet was simply out of the question, especially as I had a full day before me, sitting in court in the morning to hear lawsuits and sailing in the afternoon. I arrived at the wing of the old Pharaonic palace set aside for me and found no attendants. My chamberlain, a predecessor of Castor, looked sheepish and started muttering under his breath. I pushed open the door to my chamber angrily – anger unbefitting a recent god! – and my nostrils were assailed by an odour of perfume, delicate and fragile, and I heard the faint melody of a harp. Standing shyly with eyes lowered was an apparition in transparent pleated white gauze. Her hair was dressed in turquoise and gold, as was her slender neck. The face... how can I catch the essence of skin and bone? Prostrate and crippled as I am, I still remember how my blood surged and my heart seemed to pound aloud like thunder! She bowed very very low and removed my boots, offering her body without words, a priestess to a god. I went mad, drunk with the smell, the colour, the texture and touch of her silken body. That act of love was a sacrificial offering, a ritual rebirth, a descent into the underworld and a flight into heaven, a walk in the Elysian fields, a stroll in the gardens of Hesperides. The rhythm was both the smooth flow of the Nile and the tidal wave of the rough northern sea. Her embrace was the night and the day; a cool spring of water running through glens strewn with ferns. I must have wept and laughed and sung out loud as she whispered, 'My lord, my adored, my love, my god. I shall worship thee forever. I shall recite for thee a thousand incantations at dawn before the shadows flee and in the twilight I shall sing a thousand poems in your praise.'

'Tell me your name, my ethereal one, my love,' I said.

'Nefertari,' she whispered.

'Isn't that the name of the beloved wife of Ramses?' I ventured, but she put her hand over my mouth to silence me and stretching herself beside me, she began to sing. I looked into her eyes and recoiled with shock, for I was looking into the green slanting eyes of a cat. She felt the vibrations of my shock, and gathered me to her. Her embrace swept away all my wounds and scars. Her lullaby drained the harshness from my limbs, and my body relaxed. Before me arose visions of beauty, and the universe took me to its heart. On her lips I tasted joy and drank the nectar of the gods. I was bathed in a languid happiness and shed layers of myself, like petals falling from a flower.

Lulled by her song, I dozed. Then suddenly my arms felt a slimy smoothness. I opened my eyes and saw a black cobra in my arms. I screamed such screams not befitting a Roman emperor let alone a god - screams of the fish market; I have had an uncontrollable aversion to snakes since I was a child. It was a military secret, carefully guarded by my staff, officers and companions, something we could not allow the soldiers to see, especially in a desert full of vipers. Imagine how the camp would react to see their commander-in-chief hysterical before a snake.

My screams awoke the chamberlain, my aides, the secretariat, the guards, the tribunes on duty, even the cooks and the maids came swarming to my chamber. 'The cobra, the black cobra!' I continued to scream. 'There is no cobra, my lord,' they said in chorus. An aide whispered in my ear, 'Don't forget my lord, Egyptians worship snakes. They paint them all over their bloody tombs and as their ruler, your words touch a sensitive nerve.' I looked around, my eyes glazed. 'Where did she go?' I meant Nefertari, but they thought I meant the cobra. 'There is no cobra, or anything else in your chamber, my lord.' I dismissed them, threatening the tribune with court martial.

'I assure you, Caesar,' said the pale trembling tribune, 'no one entered your chamber last night. I stood all night with my detachment before the entrance.' I waved him away, and held my throbbing temples in my hands muttering, 'This must be the initiation they speak of.' I had missed it in Eleusis, for I had misgivings at the last minute, but here in Egypt I had undergone it, like it or not. She gave me everything in one night, life in a microcosm, ecstasy and deception, adoration and fear, spiritual heights and the void. Perhaps that is how a god perceives things, and she adored me as a god. I looked around the bed recess. There was no perfume, no music, only a Roman Emperor in his fifty-fifth year who, for a moment, had regained his youth and felt eternal; A man who had spent life in frugal austerity on far-flung battlefields under sun and rain, who had briefly enjoyed the luxury of all the senses, all the colours, all the sounds, blended in the one and only Nefertari; an emperor who insisted on chastity, who had ignored the laws against adultery which he had decreed, the supreme magistrate making mockery of his own laws.

I felt enraged by Egypt and the crafty priests who had made a fool of me by recognising me as a god; descendants of the same priests who had fooled Alexander the Great more than five centuries before by recognising him as the son of Amun Zeus in the oasis of Siwa. He became Alexander of the horns on his coins, and I, Severus, acquired the four locks of Serapis on mine. Egypt always wins, whatever any conqueror may think. However, my rational side was aware that I had been under deep hypnosis and the visions of heaven and hell that opened before me the night before had been pure illusions so I resumed my duties and took the opportunity of being in Upper Egypt to inspect the lines of defence, especially on the route to the Red Sea. Moving from one miserable hamlet to another along the frontier, I was appalled by the poverty of the peasants. I had not seen such poverty in any other province of the empire. I harangued the local administrators who were squeezing the life out of these undernourished wretches. One or two of the officials accompanying me had the effrontery to say, 'Caesar, they are resigned to this fate and they are happy. Look at their smiling faces." I ordered the officials to abstain from food for three days and then to tell me how resigned *they* were to hunger – if not disease.

Before I sailed to Lower Egypt, I instructed the governor to see that the burden of maintaining my suite should not fall to the native population[14].

The visit to Egypt was like a prism, showing me a different facet each day. It made me aware of my ignorance and avid for more knowledge than I possessed.[16] I saw something of antiquity, unfamiliar animals and strange places like the great labyrinth near Lake Moeris with its covered courtyards and 3,000 chambers.[17] But of greatest interest to me was the visit to the Serapeum of Memphis, the original home of the cult of Serapis, the Egyptian Osor-Hapi to whom I was devoted. At the Serapeum I re-enacted the ritual of death and resurrection, for which I was partially prepared by Nefertari in that magic night at Aswan, and of which I did not understand the significance at the time. The acclamation of 'Eis Zeus Serapis' is still ringing in my ears.

The attributes of Serapis are not only those of Serapis-Zeus-Jupiter. He is also equivalent to Osiris and Hades. He has synthesised the Osiris tradition with Dionysus, is equivalent to the sun god of Syria and has the qualifications of Aion, master of time and eternity.[18] The God in whose guise I was portrayed[19] implied eternal life for my dynasty and the promise of a new golden age.

The tour of the town of Memphis intrigued me. Fortunately, Ptolemy V had been wise enough to order it to be left truly Egyptian.[20] I vowed to keep it so, and not to have it fall victim to Roman town planners and engineers who usually rush into conquered cities and start destroying, reshaping, and building; changing the native aspect of the town and putting the Roman stamp on it. Such has been the fate of cities like Carthage, Leptis, Palmyra and Petra

After my tour of Lower and Upper Egypt, I returned to Alexandria where I found a mountain of administrative and judicial work awaiting me. Since its conquest Egypt had been neglected by Rome and I had to reorganise the administration. My first act was to give the Alexandrians a senate, for unlike most Roman towns they were without one. Augustus had refused them such a body, like the Ptolemids before us.[21] I also gave Alexandrian citizens the right to enter the Roman senatorial order if they were qualified.[22] I heard petitions and lawsuits during my year in Alexandria, and, assisted by Plautianus and my judicial staff, I formulated decrees in response to the many enquiries. I had these decrees published in Alexandria in Latin and Greek, and many of the Alexandrian laws I changed.[23]

The highlights of my year in Alexandria were the frequent visits to Alexander's tomb. Augustus, as Suetonius tells us, visited the tomb, and after a long look at the great conqueror's features, showed his veneration by crowning his head with a golden diadem and showering flowers on the grave.[24] Hadrian also visited the tomb. I usually entered the tomb alone and had the doors closed behind me. How often did I stand there mesmerised, facing the youth with his waxen face, dead for five centuries; and yet the skill of the embalmers who had been rushed to Babylon had almost brought him back to life. I could see the shadow of a smile on his unmoving lips, and his profile from the angle where

I stood was the most perfect I have ever seen; the body was slight and his hands had the long tapering fingers of an artist, not those of a rough warrior like mine.

There was something magical in his presence and I had the irrational belief that if I waited long enough the youth would make a sign or raise an eyebrow or speak. The sight of such beauty brought tears to my eyes and yet this pale young man with the hands of an artist and the soul of a philosopher had achieved conquests beyond my dreams. He reached India and ordered Niarchos, his fleet commander, to prepare the conquest of Arabia, while I, with my thirty-three legions, was given a triumphal arch on reaching Ctesiphon, a city on the fringe of the worlds he conquered. How I felt his presence on my passage through deserted Babylon, the cursed city where the god-king died. The irony is that I, tough old warrior, thought I had achieved wonders by planting a Roman garrison at Nisibis or Europos but the descendants of Alexander's veterans still live in Bactria and the Indus valley! I am not ashamed to admit that I wept for the delicate youth, the maker of dreams; generation after generation still live on broken elements of his vision. I am proud that I share his dream of fusing east and west, for his vision has joined the best in the Hellenic spirit with what is most noble in the east and Hellenistic cities thrive in Europe, Asia and Africa. I, like other Roman Emperors before me, have cherished and protected these manifestations of Alexander's dream.

Both Alexander and I are officially sons of Amun-Ra for on becoming Egyptian rulers, we became Pharaohs, sons of the chief god. We also share Hercules, for Alexander equated the Tyrian Melquart with Hercules. This special honour to the god of Tyre shows that Alexander must have taken the Tyrian god to be his own ancestor.[25] Needless to say, I have also been identified with Hecules–Melquart, patron god of Leptis, which was founded as a colony of Tyre. Herodotus tells us that the Egyptians also had a god named Heracles and he describes the temple of the Tyrian

Heracles with its two pillars, one of gold, one of emerald. The temple was as ancient as Tyre itself and that city stood for 2,300 years.[26]

Plautianus, worried about my frequent visits to the tomb, insisted on coming with me, but I refused. When I found tourists and pilgrims invading the tomb with their vulgar curiosity I had them kicked out. I wanted no one but myself to look at his beautiful face and I thought he needed a rest from those gawping faces and idiotic remarks. When I visited him for the last time I stayed so long that the guards panicked and knocked at the door, thinking some evil had befallen me. I ordered them out and looked lovingly at his half-smiling lips and half-opened eyes. I raised the glass and kissed his waxen forehead. I murmured my farewell with such sorrow in my heart for a life so brutally cut short, for the unfulfilled dream, for the longing that he felt for the new, the extraordinary, the unknown[27], and I promised him rest for I was the last person to see his embalmed body.[28] I sealed the tomb and instructed my chief engineer that it should be closed and hidden in such a way that no one would ever find it.[29]

Like streams and rivers that run underground, the masses have deep emotional currents buried in the darkness of their collective soul. No one could have foreseen the eruption of feelings in Alexandria after I closed the tomb of Alexander.

On learning of the closure and disappearance of the tomb the whole town, with the exception of the Jewish quarter, went into mourning. You would have thought that Alexander had died yesterday, not five hundred years before. The Greeks lamented their countryman for three days and nights. Their former rulers, the Ptolemies, had used the body of Alexander for their own political ends and encouraged this devotion to legitimise their dynasty. Many others had made use of Alexander's remains and memory: Greeks and Romans, emperors and generals had tried to imitate Alexander. Even the imbecile Niger posed as a new Alexander. The Egyptians, fed on the glory of Alexander by the Ptolemies, surpassed the Greeks in mourning. They went to such extremes that I ordered patrols to prevent foolish and desperate suicides. They made a wax effigy of Alexander and put it on a boat-shaped hearse drawn by oxen. A priest officiated, facing the effigy, and behind the hearse followed mourners and servants bearing articles for the tomb. A female impersonating Roxane, Alexander's wife, knelt before the hearse. Anubis supported the effigy and a priest read the funeral service from a papyrus. To the right of the hearse they erected a wooden replica of Alexander's tomb.[30] For three days the procession passed underneath my windows in the governor's palace, as I stood fascinated, saddened that I had obliterated the burial site for ever and made Alexander the Great die twice. In the evenings, both Greek and Egyptian quarters were lit by torches, with priests and priestesses processing to the site from which the sealed tomb had vanished. The only quiet quarter in Alexandria was the Jewish one. Alexander was neither their king nor their god, for Jehovah is a jealous god and does not admit any other. A delegation of rabbis and merchants came to see me with broad smiles on their faces. 'Congratulations Caesar on closing the tomb, for there was a sacrilegious cult around it; we are the only citizens who approve your action and are certainly not shedding any tears over the disappearance of Alexander's tomb.'

I answered them mockingly, 'Come gentlemen, Alexander the Great is worth a tear in his own city, don't you think?' And with that I dismissed them, repulsed by that air of righteousness they so often assume.

I let the Alexandrians weep; it was a collective catharsis which dried up for a while the river of anger against me that ran in each of them. I hoped that it would keep them quiet for a while at least, but I was wrong. The resentment rose again, more violently than before, when they found out from the priests that I had collected books of secret lore[31] from the tomb. Word spread like wildfire that I had also collected books of prophecy, divination and magic from sanctuaries all over the country and suppressed the Ptolemaic oracle of the potters, which had foretold the destruction of foreign rulers.[32]

They attributed my actions to fear of Egyptian magic and were outraged at the loss of the secret and sacred books collected by their priests since time immemorial. They knew about my obsession with prophecies and divination but did not appreciate my curiosity about everything, including things that have been carefully hidden and matters both human and divine.[33] But sealing the tomb and collecting the sacred books were only the prelude to a singular act which I must divulge now that my time is near. It is that I never let anyone's eyes fall on the secret books I collected. I wanted to decipher them all alone, but the bulk were in hieroglyphics and I did not want to call upon the priests to interpret for me; they were outwardly servile towards me but resentful in their hearts and I wanted to keep my distance. But to my great joy, I found greek translations of books I took from Alexander's tomb, which must have been made for one of the Ptolemies.

I spent my nights alone, bent over the Greek texts, and learned that the power possessed by a priest or one with knowledge of magic was believed to be almost boundless. By pronouncing certain words or names of power in the proper manner and in the proper tone, a priest could heal or cast out evil spirits, and could restore the dead to life.[34]

What a revelation! All my life I had been looking for such a priest or such a man, and without a second thought I sent a detachment of soldiers to the Iseum of Alexandria to bring to me the chief priest of Isis, Nefer-Uben-b; for the goddess Isis, I learned from the texts, possesses wondrous magical powers of life and death.[35] I also learned that a specialist with knowledge of magical formulae, armed with amulets and talismans, who knows how to use the 'double house of life' library of magic books –which I now possessed – can, after the recital of certain formulae, restore a body in the tomb to the form he once had when alive.[36] I was staggered by the power contained in these books and could well appreciate the shock of the Egyptians when I appropriated them.

The priest of Isis arrived while I was deep in these thoughts. The bent old man looked very frightened at the midnight summons. I dismissed everybody and asked him to be seated. I poured him a glass of wine from my imperial vineyards year Oea, nectar of the gods. I made small talk, asking after priests I had known at the Serapeum and Iseum and when he began to relax I gently explained to him my request. When I had finished, there was a long stunned silence. The old man started to cough and choke with wheezing noises from his throat. I took the cup from his trembling hands and looked at him intently. 'All I ask is in your books, what you call the "double house of life". It is a practice that has been going on in Egypt for more than a thousand years and now you pretend you are shocked!'

'Great Caesar,' the priest whispered, 'I don't know how to take your request. Before you honoured us with your visit, you sent instructions to the prefect denouncing divinations and magic. The prefect sent us the instructions and I quote your words: "Simple and ignorant people must be protected from dangerous inquisitiveness about the future, whether practised by oracles or through the magic arts." You gave one year of grace after which the penalty for magic would be death, and you concluded, "send in fetters for judgement anyone contravening the regulation."[37] He started to cough so badly that I had to give him another drink, and then he said feebly, 'Forgive me, Caesar, but by this request you may be laying a trap for me to test my adherence to your decree.'

I laughed uncontrollably, while Nefer-Uben-b looked hurt and scandalised. He must have thought that such mirth did not become an emperor and that I was laughing at him. I calmed myself and said, 'High and reverend priest of Isis, I laughed because you have invoked my own decree against me, and I must admit you are only the second person ever to do that. My wife, the empress, constantly invokes my morality laws against me but I don't know if I can forgive you for accusing me of duplicity.' I continued, laughing, "Maybe you think that I should be loaded in chains for breaking the law, but may I remind you that I issued these instructions against the powers of darkness and practioners of the black art. You yourself are aware of the clever men who take advantage of the ignorance of the populace and who claim knowledge of the supernatural and power over gods, spirits and demons. My decree, revered high priest, was against the sorcery, demonology and witchcraft practiced by these associates of the devil and servants of the power of darkness.[38] I did not prohibit white magic practised by priests or men enlightened by years of prayer, which is the essence of Egyptian religious belief.'

The priest replied slowly, 'Great Caesar, you are a devotee of Serapis, incarnate of Osiris-Apis, the great god of the Egyptian underworld. In him are united the attributes of Osiris, Khent, Amenta and Dis.[39] You know what you ask is in the domain of Osiris-Pluto-Isis and Persephone, whose powers are great in the regions under the earth.'[40]

I cut him short, trying hard to control my mounting anger. 'When you mounted a campaign against me for removing the books from the temples, you did not realise that I knew it was a sham, for the originals and more copies of these books are in the tombs and I did not open or loot a single tomb. Besides, you are denying me what you willingly performed for the Ptolemid kings, particularly the recalling of the dead on a regular basis. And don't tell me they were your national kings, for you know that they did not have one drop of Egyptian blood. They married their own sisters to keep what they called their racial purity. Or have you forgotten, my friend, the difference between a request from a degenerate client king and that of a Roman Emperor?'

Chastened, the priest bowed his head and said, 'What you ask for, Caesar, the recall of your mother from the dead, can only be performed by one special priestess of Isis, who lives in a remote hamlet on the Nile. She can vivify by means of formulae and words of power properly recited, any figure made in the form of man or animal. The words of her prayers can turn pictures into realities and drawings into substance, but I cannot divulge to you any more details. I will come back for you after midnight three nights from now. I have to send word to the priestess and on my return to the Iseum I will send you incantations and recitations translated into Greek which you must repeat four times at sunset and sunrise. Incense must burn in your chamber at all hours and you must anoint your body, including your hair, with an unguent which I will send to you immediately. In addition, on the first day you will anoint yourself with cedar oil, on the second day with olive oil and on the last day with a special unguent made from the perfumes of Arabia. Meanwhile, as you will partake in the whole act, you have to be ceremonially pure, washed clean, and for three days you must not eat meat, fish, sauces, butter, cheese or cakes. Intercourse with women is forbidden; chastity is of prime importance.'[41]

These instructions amused me greatly, especially 'washed clean'; for the ancient Egyptian who gave them was clearly ignorant of the noblest Roman institution, the bath, or of the Roman mania for bathing. As to food, there was no difficulty as I rarely indulge in rich food. And as to chastity, I have always exercised self-restraint[42] and my morality laws, which my critics call excessive, prove it.[43]

The old man continued after a few moments of silence. 'The priestess will prepare a wax figure of your dead mother. Is there any particular physical mark you wish to mention?'

'No,' I said, 'except that she was of medium height, slender with auburn hair and was very beautiful.' The priest looked me up and down and I could guess what was going through his mind, for I am of small stature with black hair. He was wondering perhaps why I had not inherited my mother's beauty.

I arranged with the priest to sail in his boat, for he deemed it unwise to use the royal barge. For three days I kept to my chamber. I followed the instructions to the letter. I recited from the hymn of Osiris, 'Homage to thee, Osiris, lord of eternity, king of the gods, whose names are manifold, whose forms are holy. Thou art the soul of Ra, his own body.'[44] The second day I recited incantations from the hymn to Ra, the sun god. 'Homage to thee, O thou glorious being, O thou beautiful being, thou dost renew thyself in thy season in the form of the disc. Therefore in every place, every heart swelleth with joy at thy rising forever.'[45] For the third day, it was again to Osiris: 'O thou who are in the kingdom of the dead, the lord of everlastingness who traverseth millions of years in his existence.'[46] The long incantations became so fixed in my memory that after all these years I can still remember these fragments.

Solitude, little nourishment and the freedom from the drudgery of examining lawsuits, making decisions and answering letters, made my body lighter and my mind clearer. I told my chamberlain that I would be going on a two-day inspection tour alone and incognito. I knew that the praetorian prefect would object strongly on security grounds but I was not in the mood for banalities. I was already on another plane of existence. I imposed silence on my valet and my chamberlain and was ready to depart.

I left the palace through a back door, wrapped in my old cloak. The priest and his boat were on time. He was accompanied by one attendant and requested silence all the way up the Nile. We disembarked at last on a desolate strip on the western bank of the Nile and I was led along a tortuous path until we came upon a large sycamore tree with a few scattered huts around it. We entered one of these huts, dark but for one oil lamp. The priest signalled for me to be seated, waved farewell and left with his attendant.

When my eyes got used to the dark I saw a clean pleasant room opening into another, with stairs that led down, probably to a basement. There was a delicious smell of aromatic plants and incense. I recognised the aroma as that of the rarest incense from the hinterland of Arabia. In one corner of the room I perceived a crone, literally hundreds of years old, crouching in a corner and, beside her, a sleek grey Egyptian cat, eyes shining in the gloom. The hag, who ignored my presence, was holding a figure in her hands and her lips were moving. I realised that she was repeating words of power that could make the figure perform evil acts or good acts.[47] I also guessed that by pronouncing the words in the proper manner and tone, she could restore the dead to life. I heard her muttering, 'Thou shalt cause the form of the deceased to come forth from every hall and from the seven halls of Osiris.'[48]

When she saw that I was listening, she rose and came towards me with a cup in her hand. 'Take this potion, beloved of the gods,' she said, and smiled at me with her gaping toothless mouth. Her face was so ugly I averted my eyes. I obeyed and soon fell asleep. When I opened my eyes I was looking into the eyes of the cat. I took her in my arms and stroked her silken fur. The hag quickly handed me another potion and said, 'You will go to sleep while we recite prayers on your behalf.' I drank just to be rid of her and lost consciousness of myself and of the world around me. I felt fragmented into thousands and thousands of pieces. I was the cat, the air, the trees, the fire, the priest, the hag and the sea. The vision of the sea so disturbed me with longing that I must have jerked my body violently, for I felt a steadying hand on my shoulder and I opened my eyes to see the lovely face of Nefertari. She put her hand over my mouth as I began crying, 'Cobra! Cobra!' Was it an hallucination? Was I dreaming? 'Nefertari, Nefertari,' I cried, unable to take my eyes from such beauty. 'Why did you leave me that night in Philae?' With a voice that was music, she said, 'Oh, my lord, my beloved, you have a short memory! I received you in this room only yesterday.' At that, I spat out all the crudest obscenities I had picked up from soldiers all over the empire and all the curses I could

muster on my own. 'You cannot be the toothless old crone!'
I said. She laughed like tinkling bells. 'Yes, I am she; she is
one of many faces, but I don't want to frighten you. I have
myriad bodies, voices and lives, past, present and future.' I
cut her short. 'This is as far as it goes. Now come here and
tell me what it is all about.' Automatically, I found myself
searching for my sword. I could have killed her.

'Oh, my beloved, only one of you is Septimius Severus
Caesar, the Roman Emperor. The others of you are not for
me to divulge and in this underworld you are seeking you
are no more a Caesar than that cat!"

I looked around but the cat had vanished, and I
screamed, 'Are you also the cat?' And with that I broke
down, for I realised that I had entered a world beyond my
comprehension, beyond logic, beyond order. Again, she read
my thoughts. 'Great Caesar, you have requested entry to the
underworld; do not give up for we are almost there.' She
came near and took me in her arms and began to sing a
lullaby, very very low. I closed my eyes as she rubbed a
perfume of roses and jasmine on the palms of my hands
until I, Septimius Severus, was no more, but was hovering
between a state of being and unbeing, and the self that had
the façade of the Roman Emperor began to dissolve until
the gods judged that nothing of me remained to hinder my
entry into the domain of Persephone, Pluto, Serapis and
Osiris. I was dimly aware that Nefertari had carried me
down the staircase to the basement. She left me alone in the
dark and when my foggy brain cleared I saw figures, forms
and shapes moving in the air in circles. I suddenly cried in a
child's voice, 'Mother darling, where are you?' I was
sobbing bitterly. Slowly her perfume filled the cave, perfume
concocted for her by the most sought-after *parfumier* in
Leptis, who created special fragrances for high-born ladies
and whose secret recipes went back to Sidon. I began to cry,
'Mother, mother,'

'I am here my child,' she said sweetly as her vision rose
before me. She was wearing a white robe with a blue

translucent jewel on her shoulder,- a jewel recalling the sea. She extended her arms and I rushed to her. 'Don't come near me, my child; I am only a shadow and there is a veil between us. Oh, I miss you so my darling.'
'Fulia, Fulia.' I whispered the name I called her as a baby, being unable to pronounce Fulvia. I tried to enter her open arms but she said gently, 'What you see, my darling, is only a faint reflection of me across space and time.'
'What is to become of me, Mother?' I said, regaining the voice of a man.
'Your destiny, my darling, was worked out long before you were born, but there are always possibilities of shifts and changes. What worries me is the balance of your actions. I can see your acts in the future.' She lapsed into silence.
'Horrible acts that I have not yet committed?' I asked, in agony.
'You have embarked on a perilous course by taking the sacred books of divination. These books of the 'double house of life' are for those versed in lore inherited from generation to generation entailing lifetimes of meditation and prayer. To their adepts the future is as well known as the past, and neither time nor distance can limit the operation of their power. I am afraid for you, darling. It is not for every man to know the mysteries of life and death. It is not for you, Lucius, to draw aside the veil which hides the secrets of fate and destiny from the knowledge of ordinary mortals.'[49]
'But, Fulia, Fulia, I am...'
'No darling,' she cried. 'Do not say it. You are an ordinary mortal and the knowledge beyond the veil is beyond your comprehension; it shatters...it kills!'
I was sobbing like a child. 'Darling, darling,' she cried. 'You have called me and I did not come to cause you pain. You have so much in your favour. I look at your balance sheet. You have administered justice impartially, you have leaned towards the poor and the oppressed, you have

protected minors[50], you have protected women[51]. Your reign, my darling, is the great age of Roman jurisprudence. You have humanised the law.'

'Fulia,' I cried, 'have you come to judge me?'

'No, no, my darling, it is only for the gods to judge; but the sensitive boy that took refuge in my arms has relieved so much suffering. They don't know you, my little one, those who call you cruel and insensitive. You have brought prosperity and felicity to many. You have stood for life against death by prohibiting abortion[52], and I hope that in the eyes of the gods your good deeds will outweigh the innocent blood you have shed.'

'You too, Fulia, even you!' I said, heartbroken. 'You forget that to achieve security and prosperity for the empire I had to destroy three so-called emperors. You blame me for the eastern campaigns? I did not invent war; it is part of the human condition, and have you forgotten how I have been betrayed?'

'I gave you life, my darling,' she said in a shaking voice in which I detected sobs. 'Do not take away life from others.'

'Fulia, Fulia, you were the first to betray me; you left me too early and I missed your compassion, your love.'

'The gods willed that I leave your plane of existence. Why, I do not know. My darling, beware of prying into the secrets of fate and destiny. Your path ahead is full of surprises.'

'Fulia, tell me what to do!' I said in a fury.

'Do not meddle in the destiny of others. Do not thrust your hands into the fire, as you did when you were a baby.'

'But, Mother darling, how can I run the empire without meddling, without changing, without reconstructing?'

'Hush, my little darling. You must build instead of destroying. Preserve life instead of taking it. Your cup is full of sorrow, but the cup of sorrow will be swept away in the river of time, Lucius.'

'Fulia,' I cried, 'I toil, I build but there is nothing, only the emptiness, the void.'

'Little darling, only love can fill the void.'

Her voice and figure began to fade. I barely heard her say, 'Lucius, darling...' and then there was nothing. When I came to myself, I was in the boat between the priest of Isis and his acolyte who were holding my feet and arms to restrain my violent movements. One of them forced a drink through my lips. I looked at their stony faces and said to the chief priest, 'This is an order. Tell me what I said when I was unconscious.' The priest turned to his acolyte, who said, 'My lord, you were sobbing and groaning, calling, "Fulia, I want to tear the veil," and then "Nefertari, where are you? Nefertari, come back in whatever form you wish, only come back.' I raised my hand and he stopped. I looked away from them to the river and spoke no more until we reached the back door of the palace where I only said, 'Farewell.'

SIX NIGHT

Felicitas Temporum

Eboracum (York)
3 February AD *211*

Once in the life of every man the gods, at their pleasure or caprice, accord a moment of felicity. To me, in my fifty-seventh year, plagued with disease and after years of traversing arid desert zones, was granted an oasis of greenness and running water. During that period, so long ago, I still believed in happiness. I was the master of the world. My people's happiness depended on me, and I offered them a new golden age.

The future I was proposing to the empire was rosy, constant, sure. Audaciously, vainly, I imposed my will on everyone and everything. I was blind to the jealousy of the gods. The Egyptian priests had flattered me to such a degree that I almost believed myself invincible. How can I now judge myself? But then, everything seemed possible. Maybe I was a different man!

Back in Rome after a long absence, I found myself, for a change, popular. The senate, the aristocracy and the *plebs* seemed to enjoy a sense of well-being which they attributed to me. The conservatives felt pride in the supremacy of Roman arms and the extension of the empire in the east. They, like me, believed that eternal Rome should rule the world and bestow on conquered barbarians the benefits of Roman law and justice, prosperity through newly built roads, improved agriculture and secure commerce under the protection of the legions. But I believed that Roman rule is more; it is a higher standard of living, good water and improved hygiene. The hovels in the barbarian north and the crowded cities in the east with their narrow allies and closed spaces, blossomed into cities with forums, colonnaded streets, baths and theatres. Rome offered a new way of life. Aristocrats and *plebs*, after years of uncertainty and pessimism, could look forward to a new golden age, with a stable Antonine ruling house the guarantor of prosperity and peace. How ashamed they must have been of their previous derision and criticism!

I enjoyed this benevolent climate and decided to reward the people's new loyalty by celebrating the tenth anniversary of my reign (9th April AD 202). Some years before, I had disappointed the public by not accepting the triumph offered by the senate after the fall of Ctesiphon, for I was already by then suffering from gout and unable to stand in a chariot for hours. So now, I offered the public a victory festival of seven days[1], with celebrations to suit every taste. To every Roman citizen on the grain dole and to every member of the praetorian guard, I gave ten gold pieces, one for every year of my reign. My largess cost me a total of two hundred million sesterces, a sum never before given by an emperor to the people.[2]

During the festival, seven hundred wild and domesticated beasts were killed. A structure in the amphitheatre was built to resemble a boat, which suddenly fell apart and disgorged bears, lions, panthers, ostriches, wild asses and bison.[3] I also gave victory games for which I summoned musical performers from every quarter. Mock battles were staged.[4] The people responded by offering dedications and statues to me and to my family all over the empire, especially in Africa.[5] I used the occasion to bestow the *toga virilis* on my son Geta[6], and to celebrate the wedding of my fourteen-year-old son Bassianus Antoninus to Publia Fulvia Plautilla[7], the daughter of Plautianus, whom I love like a daughter. I bestowed on her the title of 'Augusta', for my son is co-emperor, and the title appears on her coins and inscriptions.[8]

The marriage was celebrated with great splendour and Plautianus gave his daughter a dowry equal to the dowries of fifty women of royal rank. The gifts were seen by all being carried through the forum to the royal palace. The banquets were such as had never been seen before in Rome, being partly royal and partly barbaric in style.[9] The marriage made me very happy for now I could look forward to having an heir to the throne, and Plautilla is graceful and well-educated. She is of my mother's family and it gives me pleasure to have again united a Septimii and a Fulvii.

My happiness was only fleeting, alas, for I did not count on the dark side of the moon, and Julia was given the attributes of the goddess of the moon identified with Caelstis Ourania.[10] From the very start, she was categorically opposed to the marriage, not only because she hated Plautianus whom she accused of infiltrating the imperial house through his daughter, but also because she wanted for her son a young bride from the Roman aristocracy with an impeccable pedigree. She gave me a list of illustrious well-bred beauties, who included some girls from our family, grand-daughters of Marcus Aurelius and others of yet more noble and ancient stock. She asked me viciously, 'Is it the fortune of Plautianus that you covet? The wealth that you yourself showered on the pauper?' She pointed out the advantages to the dynasty of a Roman marriage instead of a Punic one, but she well knew that where Plautianus was concerned I was not susceptible to reason, and she told me plainly that I was completely under his thumb. When she failed to convince me, she said, 'Have you no affection for your son? You know that he loathes Plautilla.' And she asked my permission to call him. Antoninus was more adamant than his mother; he raged against Plautianus and his daughter; he called her a shameless creature, ill-bred and dissolute. Mother and son stood shouting opposition to my project and I was provoked to one of those fits of anger which I had experienced only a few times before, and with disastrous results. By the time I had finished with them, Julia and her son were on their knees begging forgiveness. I ordered them out of my sight, chastised and humiliated. The wedding took place and Julia played her part as empress, not as mother. Antoninus' hostility to his wife showed itself clearly after their wedding night. He refused to eat or sleep with her[11] and threatened to kill Plautilla and her father once he became emperor. All this, of course was reported to Plautianus.[12]

The situation between me and Plautianus became uneasy. I caught him looking at me reproachfully with his hooded eyes, and his police reports about the conduct of Julia and her son became intolerably obnoxious. One day he exasperated me so much with his constant reproaches, that I had to tell him quietly, 'You know that I forced Antoninus to marry your daughter, but I cannot force him to sleep with her!' Plautianus left my office like a raging bull. I was so angry I called him back and said, 'What about my hopes for an heir to the throne? What about those coins I issued on their marriage with the legend, *propago imperii*?[13] Do you think you are the only injured party? Why don't you leave them alone for a while and stop inciting your daughter against her husband.'

I did not brood on the situation, hoping that it would resolve itself. I had coins issued showing Plautilla Augusta clasping hands with her husband, and the legend '*concordia*'[14], in the hope that the relationship between them would improve. I blindly refused to admit my mistake, or see the elements of tragedy lurking inside the palace. How often in the moments between sleeping and waking do I see Plautilla, with her sad drawn face floating around the corridors of the palace decked in her finery and blazing with jewels, as if looking for something she had lost? I implored Julia to be kind to her because, in my cowardice, I could not bear to talk to my son on the subject. How many nights have I spent here in Britain thinking of her fear and wretchedness, of her disgrace, of her lonely exile on the island of Lipari where I sent her and her brother?[15] I hear the ghost of her father whispering in my ear, 'Septimius, what did you do to my daughter and to my son? You know that he will kill them when you die. I beg you send them away for safety to Armenia, to Parthia where he will not be able to reach them.' And I, knowing my son, hesitated and hesitated; and now as my hour approaches, I leave the beloved children of Plautianus to their fate.

In AD 203, soon after the celebrations of the *decennalia* and the mariage, the triumphal arch was inaugurated. It is a grandiose construction with a height of twenty-three metres and it took eight years to complete. Set in the north east corner of the forum, between the imperial pulpit and the senate house, in front of the temple of concord, it is in the exact spot where I had the dream which foretold my accession to power.[16] The chief architect and chief engineer visited Syria to consult me about the design, and I made it clear to them that the arch should be a symbolic monument which manifests the connection between the Parthian victory, the Severan dynasty and the continued prosperity and felicity of the Roman world.[17] The enormous inscription in gilded bronze letters enumerates my titles at the time of the official senatorial decree. Thus the titles of Parthicus Arabicus and Parthicus Adiabenicus were inscribed on the arch following literally the decree (195) and its date, while Parthicus Maximus, which I was granted later, does not appear.[18] At the bottom is the inscription 'Erected by the senate and people of Rome, on account of the restoration of the republic and extension of the empire'.[19]

It is a spreading, three bayed arch, with four great panels placed above each side of the arches, each bearing twelve scenes sculptured in relief depicting the principal episodes of the Parthian wars. The sculptures and the reliefs of the arch were carved by artists brought from Greece and Asia Minor who have mixed with classical forms a new technique of two-dimensional sculpture originating in the workshops of Aphrodisias. The artists were spread over a number of different workshops so as to complete the arch as rapidly as possible.[20] Contrary to the inscription which only refers to the first Parthian war, the reliefs combine the two wars and also show the main events of the second Parthian war, for Nisibis was the only city captured in the first campaign, while Seleucia, Babylon and Ctesiphon were captured in the second. Military historians supervised the scenes for exactitude, and I often supplied a forgotten detail like the rectangular form of Nisibis or the rounded form of Ctesiphon. In the middle zones of the arch are two river gods – one young and one old – and victory figures, twice life-size, dominate the spandrels of the central arch, bearing Parthian trophies on the ends of poles. Mars, the god of war appears with his own Parthian trophy. The iconography of the arch provides solid proof of the victory of the Roman citizenry.[21] The arch high, wide and eye-catching is like a bill-board: it advertises my exploits on behalf of Rome.

The reliefs which interest me most are those of the seasons, which appear in the lower corner of each of the four spandrels; four virginal youths who embody the happiness that followed the imperial victory. To me they are the best carvings on the whole arch, for the artists have somehow caught the impulsive eagerness of youth. A young boy for winter and a semi-nude youth for spring appear on the forum side, while on the capitol side are the figures of summer and autumn. The reliefs of the seasons celebrate the theme *felicitas temporum*: victory upon which prosperity depends. Mars and victory in the central bay are the deities who represent peace as the prize of war. The river gods in the side spandrels are symbolic of fertility.[22] The legend *felicia tempora* has appeared on the coins issued for my sons, reaffirming the imagery of the bountiful world under imperial rule.[23]

The two gods on the south east and north west keystones represent Hercules-Melquart with whom I am identified and in whose guise I am portrayed in a sculpture with the lion skin on my head in the theatre of Leptis, and the other patron of Leptis, the god Liber.[24] The two gods refer to my two sons on whose good fortune the future depends. Both gods have sovereignty over my native city and I have attached them to the Severan house as *Di Patrici* and *Di Auspices*. I have honoured them both with a temple in Rome and a medallion of bronze.[25]

My involvement with the architects and artists provided many happy days and the representation of my Parthian triumph serves to connect the historical past with the time to come. The sculptures, especially those of seaons, point to the prosperous era just beginning. I expressly asked the artists to take as models the figures of victories, river gods and seasons on the arch of Trajan at Benevento. This was appropriate as we both were associated with the *Victoria Parthica*, an anniversary celebrated in my calendar.[26] Paintings of the battles, representing those shown on the arch, were also put on public display for the people of Rome.[27] At its inauguration the monument was magnificent, with its rich detail, and fine marble in harmony with the symbolic and narrative reliefs and the play of light splendid over the mouldings and profiles. The flashing gold of the gilded inscription and the surfaces of the great relief panels, painted in gold, red, blue and green[28], had a dazzling effect on everybody.

Politically, the arch has great importance for me, as it ignores the civil wars with their horrors and uncertainty, and highlights instead victory over a foreign enemy. It has established my claim to the title *invictissimi* and represents the penance and the allegiance of the senate[29]. Above all it is a glowing testimony to the skill of the architects and artists of the empire. It is an edifice that I have never tired of looking at and now, away from Rome and knowing I will never see it again, I have a constricting pain in my heart.

The construction of the arch, paid for by the senate, whetted my appetite for building both privately at my own expense and for the state. I was perhaps obeying the words of my mother from the beyond, 'Lucius, build, build, build!'

I established workshops all over Rome, employing hundreds of architects, surveyors, engineers, sculptors and craftsmen, to repair the old monuments of Rome and to build new ones.[30] My first project was to add a wing to the corner of the Palatine Palace: the Septizodium, facing the Via Appia, is a three-storeyed building which I had modelled on the nymphaeum of Leptis[31], with a majestic façade and seven niches for the seven planets. In the centre stands the statue of the sun, sculpted in my likeness, looking towards Africa welcoming travellers from that continent.[32] I must admit however, that without Julia's pestering, I would not have undertaken the work, for she went around complaining that I repaired all of Rome save only the palace!

I also started on a huge bath complex, the Antonine Baths, on which work has been continuing for five years. It was still not completed when I left for Britain. I undertook the restoration of all the public sanctuaries in Rome which had fallen into ruin through the passage of time, and seldom inscribed my name on these restorations or failed to preserve the names of those who built them.[33] I still have on my office wall a huge map of Rome engraved in marble marked with all the sanctuaries and public buildings that needed attention.[34] Each time a monument was restored I crossed it off, until none were left. The restoration of the Pantheon was one of my priorities. Hadrian had repaired it before me, almost rebuilt it, but again the portico was crumbling. I rennovated it and used it as a model for the Porticus Octaviae which I restored in AD 202.[35]

The restoration programme was a drain on my private purse as well as on the treasury, but the reward was that Romans began to restore and build at their own expense, dedicating buildings to me. The guild of silversmiths built an arch, known as the Argentari, a monument of modest architectural quality, at the entrance of the Forum Boarium and dedicated it to me in AD 204.[36] In three years of exhilarating and intense activity, I significantly improved the appearance of Rome, but I did not forget the provinces;

I constructed public monuments at my own expense in Syria, Greece and Asia. I made a short visit to Africa in 203 and started the building programme which was to make Leptis one of the most magnificent cities of the empire.

The saecular games in 204 were the crowning glory of these years. Rome was alive with festivals and celebrations, theatrical and religious ceremonies and building programmes. For me, it was the height of public and private happiness. The games were of an expiatory nature; I hoped to attone for the sins and crimes of the old cycle and to mark a new cycle, or age of man, with solemn sacrifices. The festival of three days and nights is traditionally in honour of Pluto and Persephone, the gods of the underworld. Each cycle takes one hundred and ten years using the ancient method of Etruscan reckoning, or one hundred years following the Roman civil cycles: this ensures that nobody is alive who has taken part in the previous cycle celebrations.[37]

The games were first established as a public ritual 250 years after the foundation of Rome. Augustius revived them in AD 17[38], as the fifth of the series. The last celebration was Domitian in ad 88. The next cycle commenced in AD 198 but as I was absent in Asia, celebrations had to await my return six years later. My festival was the seventh in the series, which was most fortunate for I am attached to this planetary number. I held them at the end of May with the theme of a new golden age and a happy period for all the universe.[39] I had coins struck with the legends *Sacre Saecularia* and *Ludos Saeculares* with pictures of the special wooden theatre erected for the occasion in Campus Martius.[40] The celebrations included religious ceremonies in imitation of mysteries. Heralds travelled throughout Italy summoning the people to come and attend games the like of which they had never before seen and would never again see.[41] As tradition decreed, I appointed a board of fifteen religious advisers to perform sacrifices, and I entrusted them with the Sibylline oracles and foreign relgious rites. Among the board were those who had acquired this position from descent, but I also added some whose foreign ancestors had been granted Roman citizenship. It gave me great pleasure to appoint to this board, which represents the heart of ancient and revered Roman tradition, nine Africans. The senate decreed the duration of the festival as a public holiday. Lawsuits were postponed and women were prohibited from mourning for thirty days.[42]

I granted my wife honours greater than Augustus had given to Livia on the same occasion: I appointed Julia a priestess in the ceremonies[43] and put her in charge of the honours to the goddesses Juno and Diana, including the sacred banquets with 109 married women on the capitol.[44]

The ceremonies ended in hymns of praise to the new golden age and thanks to the imperial family as initiators of this new era.

The mere memory of this period of felicity brings a jolt of joy to my heart, and only now in hindsight can I see that the cycle was destined to end: but why, why was I so blind that I failed to see the shadows looming, the hovering darkness which destroyed my landscape, for Plautianus was the landscape wherein I dwelt.

Until I lost him, I did not realise except on a certain level of consciousness hidden from the light, that I had lost all joy. I had not been aware that what I had achieved in the past twelve years had only been possible because I lived through him in the landscape of my youth and in the earth and sky which had given me birth. He was the shade of the olive tree at high noon and the haze that sparkles over the blue of the sea. He was the thicket of bamboo surrounding the cool mountain spring, into which I dipped my hands to drink. It was to his landscape that I turned when men betrayed me, when the battle turned against me and when people murmured maledictions as I passed along the street. What malignant fate, what injustice blinded me and induced me to throw away the resting place I had in his heart?

I did not see, nor understand then, that each of us needs

a place in a corner of another being, or if of a more philosophical disposition, in religion or the beyond. Oh, yes, he was essential like the air I breathe! My pleasure doubled when he shared it, and my grief was mitigated by his slightest gesture, a look from his hooded green eyes, or an inflection in his voice. He restored my balance when my judgement slipped, and he gave me the tranquility of spirit to indulge my passion, the administration of the law. He shared the empire with me and in a secret chamber of my heart I wished him to succeed as emperor.[45] He was the younger man, the love of my youth[46]: I gave him power beyond all men[47] and yet I allowed him to die. I cannot forget his greenish eyes looking at me with dull amazement as if to say 'How could you, Septimius?' Yes, how could I? But I have received my punishment, for the wrath of the gods descended upon me, and since his murder six years ago, I have lost all capacity for joy and my passion for life.

Who would have thought that the seeds of tragedy were sown in the time of my greatest happiness? Julia, who hated Plautianus, was helpless for a long time, but after his marriage she had her son as ally. I do not really believe that Antoninus loathed Plautilla as he claimed, for it is difficult for anybody to hate such loveliness, but he despised her father; not because Julia hated him but because as praetorian prefect Plautianus controlled his conduct, his abuses, and his excesses[48] and reported all to me. My wife and son and many others knew that I yielded to Plautianus on all matters, and they even referred to me behind my back as the prefect, and to Plautianus as the emperor.[49] They called him the fourth Caesar.[50]

Antoninus and Julia found another ally in my brother Geta who was jealous of Plautianus' place at my side. I was forced to remind Geta that I had not inherited the throne and he had no rights to the succession. Geta kept silent after that and did not dare open the subject again until on his deathbed. Am I not doing the same thing in these memoirs? Perhaps it is a family trait! My dying brother told me that out of fear of Plautianus he had never dared to tell me of his infamy before.[51] It only struck me later, when I remembered what my brother had said, that I really knew nothing of Plautianus' secrets nor his inner self, while he knew everything that I said or did.[52] He did not allow anybody, not even me or Julia, ever to see his wife.[53] Plautianus wanted everything and would take everything. People sent more gifts to him than to me.[54] I allowed senators and soldiers to take oaths by his fortune, and they all publicly offered prayers for his preservation.[55] Towards all he behaved like an emperor, and he said to the senate who were passing decrees in his honour, 'Show your affection for me in your hearts, not in your decrees.'[56]

I allowed him to lodge in better places and to enjoy better food than myself.[57] I made him sole prefect after he killed his colleague, Aemilius Saturninus.[58] His statues and images – erected by individuals, countries and by the senate – are more numerous and larger than mine.[59] However, I well remember the great public resentment against him which I chose to ignore. This was most clearly shown in the circus when the populace exclaimed, 'Plautianus, why do you tremble? Why are you pale? You possess more than do the three'[60], meaning me and my sons. I pretended not to know[61] about the hundred Roman citizens of noble birth that he had castrated – grown men, some of them with wives – just so that Plautilla should have eunuchs as attendants and teachers of music and art. He emasculated bearded fathers and I did not censure him.[62] But for this alone he deserved to die. I should have suspected Plautianus long ago in Leptis when he was in humble circumstances and Pertinax, at that time pro-consul of Africa, condemned him for corrupt practices. I interceded on Plautianus' behalf and Pertinax granted me a favour by releasing him.[63] As emperor I showered vast wealth upon him, making over to him the property of those he condemned[64], but he repaid me by trying to outshine me in our home town of Leptis, claiming that he was the city's greatest son.[65]

Julia had told me about his abuse of boys and girls and about his gluttony and shameful behaviour at banquets[66], but I chose not to believe her because she was prejudiced against him. I knew, on the other hand, that my brother was telling the truth, even though I suspected that there was an understanding between him, Julia and Antoninus. I felt very guilty about the indifference and neglect I had shown towards my brother and I was sincerely ashamed of my unfounded suspicions that he wanted to succeed me. My penance came too late; the only amends I could make on his death was to erect a bronze statue to him in the forum.[67] What my brother revealed about Plautianus revolted me; it was against the dignity of his position and his office, particularly given that I had made him a senator, twice a consul and a patrician.[68] He was a *comes* (companion, a post of high honour awarded to a chosen few, in the inner circle of the emperor) and I even allowed him to have his own companions.[69] In public, I was told, he wore the broad stripe on his toga, a sword at his side, and on his person every badge of high rank. His presence was awesome; no one dared to approach him. The companions who preceded him allowed no one to stare at him; all had to stand aside and keep their eyes lowered.[70]

I was troubled. I could neither deny nor tolerate his misdeeds nor his abuse of power, but he was my kinsman[71], a Fulvii, and I loved the man so much that I prayed to die before he did.[72] However, in the meantime I simply had to react, and my first step was to keep him at a distance. I was no longer always available and his constant requests to see me added to my irritation. I ordered many of his statues to be melted down, which resulted in the rumour that he had been deprived of his posts. On hearing these stories, some demolished his images on their own authority, among them the governor of Sardinia, Racius Constans. The spontaneous reaction against Plautinius alarmed me, for I could not bear to see him humiliated or condemned, and I decided to punish all those who had destroyed his statues.

At one of the ensuing trials, the orator speaking on his behalf declared that the heavens would fall before Plautianus would suffer any harm under Severus. I was present at the trial and confirmed this statement.[73] The public aversion to Plautianus did not die however, but because I shunned him, rumours went around that I had declared him public enemy. I felt his misery and longed for his company. The equestrian Africans whom he gathered around him looked at me reproachfully, as did Plautilla. I gave in and resumed our friendship; and to demonstrate this renewal, I entered the city on horseback in his company, as if celebrating a minor triumph. To complete Plautianus' rehabilitation, I exiled all those who had declared him public enemy.[74]

Plautianus did not learn his lesson, for his demeanour and manner did not change. Modesty decorum and diplomacy simply did not exist as far as he was concerned. He attributed his temporary fall from grace to Antoninus and treated him more harshly than ever, meddling overtly in his affairs, rebuking him and controlling his actions.[75]

It was then that my son started to plot against him with the help of his mother, some freed men and the palace guards. And it was on All souls Day, the 23rd of January AD 205, feast of dead ancestors, heroes and deified emperors, that fate cruelly intervened. I was ready for dinner after the spectacle, when a Syrian centurion presented himself urgently and read a letter from Plautianus, apparently ordering him with ten other centurions to kill the two emperors, myself and my son. The suddenness unnerved me as I had dreamt the night before that Albinus was alive and was plotting against me.[76] I suspected nevertheless that my son had worked out a plan to put Plautianus to death. I sent for Antoninus and accused him of plotting against the man who was my friend and his father-in-law. He denied the charge.[77] I summoned Plautianus, as if on some business. I gave order for his bodyguard to be detained at the gate, and he entered alone. Mildly, as if enquiring about his health, I asked him: 'Why did you wish to kill us?' . He was so amazed at the accusation that he started to deny it and to defend himself by saying it was a trick, a plot to destroy him. I cut his speech short and reproached him, reminding him of the honours and benefits I had given him.[78] He in turn reminded me of his loyalty: of all the risks he had taken for me; how he had paved the way to Rome for me in 193, how he had seized the sons of Niger, to enable me to have a hold over him. He reminded me that he had intercepted Niger's letter to the senate, who otherwise would have declared him emperor before me. He then turned to me, his whole body trembling, 'I was at your side in the Parthian campaign. I was at your side in Egypt and helped you formulate the judicial decrees.[79] As prefect I have protected you and kept Rome and Italy safe for you. As to my daugher whom your son has insulted and slighted – was it really such a bad bargain for a Septimii to marry a Fulvii?'

As I stood there, ashamed of myself, with my tenderness returning, my son, suddenly frightened that I would soften, struck him with his fist. Plautianus, incredulous, murmured, 'You have forestalled me in killing.' I turned around and held Antonius back, preventing him from striking my old friend again. In that second, Antonius ordered the tribune to slay him.[80] And so it was that they killed him before me, while I stood speechless. I saw his body roll on the floor at my feet and saw one eye half opened for a moment – some life still glimmering in his prone body. He looked at me and in that second of time worlds passed by, the cycles of the whole universe whirled in my paralysed brain and the truth was revealed. He was not guilty. I was the murderer of the man I loved. I saw a tribune pluck hairs from his beard, and heard Antonius bidding him to take them to Julia and Plautilla, to the joy of one and the grief of the other. I was still frozen where I stood when I saw them throw his body from the palace window to the Via Sacra and it took me some time before I found voice enough to order them to gather him up and bury him.[81]

I could have prevented this outrage, but it is certain that some part of me wanted him dead. Standing there, dumb and mute, I knew that any pleasure I took in living had died with him forever. What a shabby plot by Antoninus and Julia! Both bore him a jealousy without bounds and they killed him because I loved him. His fall entailed disaster for all his followers and friends. Among these, Coecilus Agricola, who flattered Plautianus more than any other, was sentenced to death. He was to forestall his executioners however; he went home and having drunk chilled wine from the cup which cost him 200,000 sesterces, shattered it and cut his veins with one of the broken shards, falling dead upon the precious stones and fragments.[82]

I could not stand the abuse against Plautianus now that he was dead. I called a hasty meeting of the senate, who were waiting gleefully for me to denounce him, but instead of uttering accusations against him, I only deplored the weakness of human nature, so easily corrupted by excessive honours, and I only blamed myself that I had honoured the man and loved him so.[83]

I banished Plautilla and her brother, not only to save them from my son, but because their presence reminded me that I was a criminal; that I killed an innocent man, who in the second he was struck, looked at me astonished. Could I, who loved him so, have taken on such a heinous deed?

For days I was dazed, but I kept my composure in public. During the night I was seized with a madness. I wanted to resort to the Egyptian book of divination and prophecy to bring him back from the dead and to hear his voice once more. I planned to bring the priest of Isis from Egypt, to relive the process which had enabled me to see and speak to my mother – even though he would only have been a ghost and a veil would remain drawn between us. In the cold light of morning, however, I asked myself how a murderer would ever speak to the ghost of his victim. What could I say to the man that I loved so dearly yet had betrayed so utterly? I was certain that the ghost of Plautianus, if forced by the magic of the priests to resurface, would simply turn his eyes away from me and refuse to speak.

I have no words to describe the four years after his death, or the void that I traversed before I came to Britain, coming as it did after the Decennalia and the Saecular games when I led people, including myself, to believe in happiness and a new golden age. I could not stand living in Rome, and moved my family to Campania[84] to keep my sons from the dissolute, immoral life they led in Rome. I took them away from the company of gladiators and charioteers. But it was in vain. Plautianus used to control and moderate their conduct, but I failed.

It was high time that I turned my attention to the administration of the empire. I had to remedy the sorry state of things after Commodus and his excesses. The treasury was empty, but my confiscation of the estates of the followers of Niger and Albinus, from Spain to Syria – some of the richest in the empire –made the state a rich proprietor. It rented the land long-term to farmers.[85] I had to reorganise the fiscal structure, debase the coinage and uproot the corruption in the administration, another legacy of Commodus. The social and economic state needed adjustmemnt due to the demobilisation of large armies after the civil and foreign wars. Deserters and refugees, out of desperation, turned to lawless acts and brigandage[86] and joined the brigand, Bulla Felix. Finally I had to send in the army to stop them terrorising the country and to take measures to ameliorate the economic situation. My concern was to protect the rural population from so many obligations[87], for the structure of the state was in essence based on a militarised peasantry. One important item on my agenda was the need for urgent repairs to the road system throughout the empire, especially between Italy and the northern frontiers.[88]

As to the laws, my last years in Rome were guided by Papinian, a treasure house of jurisprudence, whom I named Praetorian Prefect after Plautianus. I named him vice president of the judicial council. This was made up of distinguished jurists such as Ulpian, a native of Tyre, and Paul. The Council issued the laws and the Senate became a court house to register its decrees.[89]

I have mentioned already the laws on the rights of women, minors, slaves, guardians of testimony and property disputes[90], but the legislation I was most proud of was the decree which rules that Punic and Celtic, or any other native language, could be used in legal documents.[91]

I also relieved the provincials from the burden of maintaining the imperial post, a privilege Italian towns had enjoyed since Nerva.[92] By such legislation I gave equality to the provinces and strengthened their identiy with a common homeland, the Roman Empire. The whole apparatus of the law with its sympathy for the protection of the weak against the mighty became a necessary duty for the governors of the provinces.[93]

My reverence for the law was demonstrated in a joint statement I issued with my son, the co-emperor: 'Although we are not bound by the law, we live in accordance with it.'[94]

SEVENTH NIGHT

Omnia fui et nihil expedit

Eboracum (York)
4 February AD 211

The dogs around the palace are howling; their baying brings memories of starry nights in Leptis. Strange how two different races of dog have similar reactions to the spectre of death. In Leptis, a collective shudder would creep through the houses, and we children would run out to guess in which house the wake could be. To us, the ritual of death with all its ceremonies was a great source of enjoyment. We ran free; nobody bothered to drive us away for our parents were too involved in the rituals. With what joy did we anticipate the chorus of Punic laments sung by women who let down their long dark hair, covered it with ashes and smeared their faces with soot from the bottoms of old pots and pans. With what glee did we watch the womenfolk hurrying to change their robes and tunics for old ones when the rumour of death made the rounds, for they were loath to be caught in new clothes. Tradition demanded that they could not enter the house of the dead without soot and ashes, and protocol demanded that they stand immobile on the threshold until seen by everyone, and then with a dramatic gesture tear their tunics from top to bottom with a loud cry.

The second and third days after the death were the climax, for that was the time for funerary dances. Women of the family and friends made a circle within a circle within a circle, and with hands crossed before their breasts, they danced slowly, scarcely moving; and then suddenly, they whirled and hopped in a frenzy, slapping their cheeks.

Nobody knew where this archaic ritual originated, but legends recount that it came with the immigrants from Sidon, Tyre and the land of Canaan; the dirges nobody understood either for they were in old Phoenician. The ceremonies lasted three days for the ordinary man, nine days for a notable and forty days for a sufete, legate, consul or senator. For me, alas, there will be no Punic maidens with long shimmering hair, dancing in circles and chanting hypnotic dirges, to accompany me on my journey across the Styx.

Julia will remember the ceremonies of her people in Emesa, a replica of those in Leptis, but she is Augusta, wife of a Roman Emperor and mother of two, and she will comply with funerary rites according to strict Roman tradition. My worn body, arrayed in military garb, will be put on a pyre, and my two sons and the whole army in full ceremonial dress will run around it to exhaustion. The soldiers will then throw their gifts on the pyre and my sons will apply the fire.[1] The sound of my soldiers' feet will be music to my ears as were their war cries when I led them into battle. Their love will ease my crossing to the other world. My rival, Albinus, was loved by the aristocracy, Niger by the *plebs*, but I have the love of the army. In fact I have lived my life as emperor, and before that as tribune and legate, in army camps, and it is there surrounded by my soldiers and their broken Latin that I have felt at home; never in the Palatine.

My mind is wandering but keeps returning to the alabaster urn that will contain my ashes. It arrived from Rome this afternoon; perfect timing! I had it placed on the chest facing my bed and I catch myself gazing at it with wonder. I ordered Castor to bring it to my bed. I caressed the translucent stone, whispering, 'Little urn, you will hold a man that the whole world could not contain.'[2]

Images of my life pass before me but no wonder, for this is my seventh and last night before the curtain falls. I chose to begin my countdown seven nights ago because the planetary number has governed all the salient events of my life and what is more important than my death? Events long imprisoned in the darkness of memory are fighting to escape, and of these a white horse with the saddest eyes in the world is the first to emerge. It was when I disbanded the praetorian guards before I entered Rome with my army. I had sent orders for them to assemble in ceremonial dress outside the city. I mounted a podium and looked upon the most splendid body of men the world knew; they stood in their impeccable uniforms with shining ceremonial daggeres inlaid with silver and gold, their heads raised, expecting to hear about the gifts which a new emperor usually makes to the guards. Instead of flattering words and donations, however, I reproached them bitterly for the part they had played in the slaying of Pertinax; their treacherous deed against the emperor they had made an oath to protect. I then pronounced the words that struck them like lightning. I disbanded them, banishing them a hundred miles from Rome on pain of death. In disbelief they reached for their arms but saw that my Illyrians surrounded them with levelled spears. How pitiful this once proud body stood, their heads bent in shame. They were ordered to take off their uniforms and throw down their arms, and slowly, in only their tunics, they started to disperse.[3]

The mounted men were told to let their animals go, but there was one man whose horse would not leave him. The praetorian stood by his horse, stroking its neck and whispering something in its ear, and then shooed it away. The horse refused to move. The soldier was perplexed; he stroked the horse again, and talked to it as if imploring it to go, and walked away. The horse followed him, trotting by his side. The praetorian, now desperate, turned to one of the Illyrian soldiers and asked for a weapon. He held the sword and stood looking at me and the officers who stood at my side as if hoping for a word of reprieve, but I was as silent and cold as a stone. He then turned to the horse, caressed its head, its flanks and whispered farewell. The horse seemed pleased to see its master handling the sword, and the praetorian turned quickly round and stabbed his faithful mount. With tears running down his face, the soldier then raised the sword and killed himself.[4] There was a deathly hush, and soldiers on both sides bowed their heads. I turned away lest anybody should see tears in the emperor's eyes. At that moment I hated myself, the empire, the throne and what I represented, for I had coldly and deliberately broken the bond between a man and his horse, a master and his best friend.   I have never forgotten the misery in the horse's eyes that turned to joy when its master raised the sword, and I who have sent thousands of loyal beautiful youths to their deaths in battlefields from Mesopotamia to Gaul have never felt such intense anguish as I felt for that beautiful horse clinging to its master until death. And now that my hour is at hand how will the gods judge me? They might perhaps forgive me all the deaths that I have caused – war is not my invention, it is part of the rhythm of things. They might even give me some credit for my humane laws. But the gods will not have mercy upon an emperor who did not himself have compassion for a faithful horse.

I can hear Jupiter banging the table before the assembled gods and saying, 'We will wait for Hercules-Melquart and for the Lady Tanit who have a special interest in the accused Septimius Severus.' He starts his speech after glowering at the late arrivals who timidly take their seats. 'My lords, my ladies, we all know we sometimes fail to understand the behaviour of mortals. Look at this fellow Severus, with an empire that extends from the Euphrates to the Rhine, from Britain to Egypt, and with a giant military machine, and yet the wretched fellow feels threatened by a dumb horse!' He laughs and the heavens shake. The rest of the assembly chuckles and giggles in derision. Jupiter then raises his hand for silence. 'You will agree, my lords and ladies, that he failed to show pity on a suffering animal, a creature also beloved by the gods. Do I hear you objecting my lord

Serapis?' Jupiter says in an icy voice. 'Come, don't mutter under your breath. Tell us openly what you think.' All the gods turn toward Serapis who says timidly, 'My lord, Severus was under great pressure; he was surrounded by enemies and he had to save the empire. In the final analysis his actions brought good to many people.' Jupiter cuts him short. 'So the good of the empire requires the misery of a poor horse, eh? What kind of an empire is that? Why don't you say, my Lord Serapis, that the wanton cruelty of Severus shows he has a heart of stone?' Jupiter stops, scrutinises the faces of the gods, cups his ears in a mocking gesture and says, 'Do I hear any more objections? Some of you are murmuring.' He fixes his gaze on Hercules-Merlquart and Tanit who lower their heads and say nothing. 'I thought not! You all agree with me that Severus shall receive the maximum punishment ever pronounced on a mortal: he will strive all his life for nothing.' And with that he taps on the table and rises majestically to signify the end of the assembly.

The memory of the horse and the imagined judgement of the gods has made my throat dry, so I call Castor for a little wine with honey and ask him to bring the doctors whom I have kept waiting for so long. The doctors' entry and their sallow faces put me in bad humour. 'Gentlemen, why this funeral look? I am not dead yet!' Their butchers' hands repel me, as do the knowing looks they exchange when I turn my head. I want to throw them out again. The worst is the know-all from Gaul and I taunt him. 'What, my dear Clovis, you do not have a new remedy today?' But then I remember their loyalty – resisting my son's bribe to poison me and his threats to execute them when he becomes emperor – and in my shame I soften and thank them for their pains and patience with a cantankerous old man. I tell them that my hour has come and that there is nothing they can do for me any more. I thank them again and bid them farewell.

Paccia Marciana beckons to me. She is waiting for me

beyond the veil. All around her is green. I don't know what Marcia does to colours, for in her presence they take on such vividness that I feel quite intoxicated. At times I catch myself looking for Marcia in the stars; the only time that my perpetual frown disappears. How they blamed me for not mentioning her in my 'official' autobiography.[5] They assumed that I didn't love my first wife; but how could I talk about her without talking about love? And that is a side I never wanted exposed to the public who believed me incapable of love, and think that I cherish my family for dynastic reasons alone. Perhaps, as some of my friends said, I didn't mention Marcia simply to avoid the jealousy of Julia. In a way that's true; I didn't want to ruffle her feathers for her bouts of jealousy can be extremely distasteful. She is jealous of the living and the dead! Early on in our marriage she would retreat into the role of the Syrian princess who had left her people for my sake, but she soon learned not to play that role, although she never let anybody forget that her Arab ancestors were priest kings. She was very hurt when the Roman aristocracy looked upon her as an upstart.

The public chose to see in me only a man whose fits of wrath were terrible, a man of cruel deeds, a man obsessed with money and with the confiscation of property.[6] My silence on my private life in the autobiography confirmed their picture of me and outraged them, for they are scandal mongers, always on the lookout for the dark secrets of the emperor and his family. If by chance there are no grounds for gossip, they invent them. I have not forgotten the stories they circulated about a liaison I was supposed to have had with a lady in the imperial circle of Marcus Aurelius.

No I didn't want to share my Marcia with the public, nor the feeling of emptiness I experienced at her loss; and now, twenty years after her death, this is the first time I have spoken of her love. Our families, the Septimii and the Marcii who were related through the Fulvii, arranged the marriage and, as rarely happens in arranged marriages, we fell in love. For ten whole years she brought my native sea breeze to me in landlocked cities. She was beautiful as only Punic women can be with olive skin, large black eyes and shining hair. She had a fragility about her which gave her an unreal quality. I was always afraid that she would vanish and constantly needed to touch her, to assure myself she was still there. What joy it was to relax on the couch after a bath while she chattered in Punic about her day. She mimicked to perfection the barbarian ladies who were trying so hard to become Roman matrons and the shrill tones of the wives of my subordinates with their condescending manners to the barbarian women. Oh, how I laughed! Just talking in Punic was a relaxation, for one's first and native language is such a comfort, especially when one is tired or stressed. How different my life would have been if it had been Marcia as empress by my side. Maybe happiness would have made me a more compassionate ruler, a milder man less prone to anger. Who knows?

We were married while I was tribune of the *plebs* in Leptis. Our clans gathered from the three sister cities of Oea, Sabratha and Leptis. For three days I lost myself in the haze of festivities and the endless banquets. There was lobster and asparagus, whole boar with truffles, peacock, mullet, fat goose livers with garlic, whole lambs on the spit and the Leptis speciality of spiced lambs' livers, wrapped with dough and baked in special ovens. It was all washed down with the finest wines of Africa, Sicily and Greece. The culmination came on the last evening when I was carried on the shoulders of my male relatives to the women's quarters, where Marcia sat enthroned. I walked towards her and slowly lifted her red veil. Why red I never knew. I looked upon a brilliant statue, for her face had been dusted with powdered gold leaf. She raised her shy eyes, and I pressed a gold coin against her forehead. This was the signal for the women to divide into two groups to sing the wedding serenade. One group sang high, the other low, and I was transfixed, for I had never heard a song of such purity. The melody came from another universe, rose abruptly and melted away. A hush came over the room. I stole a glance at Marcia, sitting by my side all golden, vibrating with the music. Her body was an instrument which promised joy. I felt I was being led straight to the Elsysian Fields and the isles of the Hesperides. Some verses of the serenade which I translated into Greek stuck in my memory; they recall that unique moment of bliss.

Into the deep and cold dark night
With no storm, wind or rain
I shall climb up to you, my love
To show my golden chain.

Far, far into the night
When the moon sets and the stars recede
I shall climb up to you, my love
To show you a love so deep.

How I wish that Punic maidens would serenade me to the nether world with the haunting songs of my wedding night. My next assignment, as legate in Lyon, came soon after the wedding, and Marcia accompanied me. Thanks to her I fulfilled my duties and never felt during my whole career beloved as in Gaul.[7] It was in Gaul that I learned the art of governing and it was there that I lost her.

The only thing left for me to do after her death was to erect a statue in her honour in Rome. I did the same for my father and mother.[8] Certain cities followed my example. In Leptis the statutes were dedicated by the community, and in the theatre by the three curies of Plotina, Nervia and Matadia.[9] Statues were also erected in Cirta.[10]

I feel refreshed by my reverie and ready for the praetorian prefect. I have told Castor to bring in the empress, my sons and the judicial council only at dawn. Here comes my good Papinian. 'Sit down my friend, for it is our last private interview, and don't look so grieved! It is true I am gasping for breath but only because I have been dictating for hours and jumping between the past and the future. Future, that is an odd word to use in this circumstance! You knew I was up to something. One cannot hide anything from you, for this is the seventh night I haven't called you in for our midnight chat.

'It is strange that in my seven nights of dictation, certain patterns running through the fabric of my life have emerged. It has taken the perspective of my approaching death to make out the woven design; to see for example my obsession with tombs, for I built the grave of Hannibal and sealed the tomb of Alexander the Great. Another pattern has emerged connecting me with Rome, for my history is hers and, believe it or not, Rome is showing the same signs of old age and decay as I am! When I came to the throne I thought I was the innovator: I set new standards, introduced new ideas and started new fashions. But my innovations now appear old-fashioned and Romans will soon feel nostalgic for my 'golden age', as they did for the republic. Take a more painful subject, my son Antoninus. I see clearly his violence, his jealousy, his suspicions and his weaknesses, but the boy would certainly have been otherwise had I shielded him from the public. Pertinax was perhaps wiser than I have been. He did not allow his children to live in the palace let alone participate in affairs of the state. I, on the other hand, made a thirteen-year-old lad co-emperor, an Augustus, and exposed him to the adulation that went with the title and position; the result is what he is now.[11] No, no, Papinian, you never flattered me before, it is not becoming to do so now. Ah, I beg your pardon, you were only quoting the oracle of Delphi, *bonus Afer*[12], the good African. That was a long time ago, when they asked the oracle to pronounce on the three rivals for the throne. You know, Papinian, throughout my life it has been justice that I sought more than goodness. You are surprised that I have spent the last seven nights dictating the story of my life, for you know me as a man of few words and many ideas[13], but the words just came out all on their own, without paying much heed to me. As you have said, I was eager for more than I obtained[14], for like Alexander the Great I have always had that longing for the unknown. I feel it more painfully now, at the doorstep of the unknown.

I would have liked to see Leptis again before I die. My last visit was eight years ago and I almost rebuilt the town. You should have seen the new forum surrounded by porticoes and shops, but the most splendid construction of all is the basilica. I approved the plan in Rome before my visit. It is an immense three-sided hall with an apse at each end, and is over thirty metres in height. The columns are a marvel. I had granite imported from Egypt and green marble from Euboea. At both ends, white marble pilasters have been beautifully carved with the adventures of Dionysus and Hercules, the patron deities of Leptis and of my family. The work has been going on for eight years. It will be finished after my death and dedicated, I hope, by my sons. You have heard about the four-way triumphal arch at the junction of the main streets which the town built on the occasion of my visit? The reliefs are very fine! Julia has come out beautifully; the artist has caught her youth and imprisoned it in the marble for ever. Work is still going on to complete the harbour extension and construct warehouses, a temple, a watchtower and a lighthouse. Sabratha rivals Leptis with its magnificent temple built by my ancestors, the Antonines, and its temples of Hercules, Liber, Pater, Isis and Serapis.[15] It was in Sabratha that I became a devotee of Serapis.

'You see, Papinian, the man of few words is talking his head off. I must have a pause and, of course, answer your questions which I see you cannot keep. You remind me of my achievements: roads built and roads repaired, granaries in Rome with a seven year supply of corn[16], olive trees planted, and what better thing can a man do than plant an olive tree? You recall to me the temples I have built and the sanctuaries I have repaired, the excesses and corruption I have eradicated and so forth; but of all of these, my good

Papinian, nothing will remain, except perhaps the laws we built together.

'I was not born under Saturn, Papinian, but like those born under that star, for me maturity came too late. The most interesting thing that my memoir has revealed is that the past itself is fluid; any one event in my past had a thousand different aspects, and as many conflicting interpretations, and if I chose one face of the prism over the others, was it, as I believed then, governed by fate? I will go to the beyond with the question unanswered. You note that the *ab epistilis graecus* is taking down my words. He will also take down yours, but all will be over at dawn.

'I have been racing against time, for how can you record a whole lifetime in seven nights? Spare me your pain Papinian. You remember I told you before we came to Britain that I knew the hour of my death. It was confirmed here in a dream.

'And now I will come to the point: I shall entrust to you this secret memoir. The Greek secretary will correct any errors in the language and then hand you two copies. One you will lodge with the vestal origins. I have already prepared a letter to the chief vestal, an old friend. The second copy is for public comsumption, but I leave with you the decision as to the most propitious moment for publication. Julia and my sons will press you to destroy the manuscript. You know as well as I Julia's obsession with power and her frustration at not sharing it with me. She will not like the revelations about my love for Marcia and Plautianus. As for my unfortunate Geta, the stars show no imperial future for him, and he would not appreciate reading of my neglect. Finally, Antoninus; you know his violent nature. He will seek to erdicate all trace of the memoir. I tremble for you Papinian, and I apologise for the burden I am laying on your shoulders, but I have no choice: There is nobody else I can trust. I still see so many questions on your face and, as yet, I have not answered two issues: why I have chosen to expose my life to the public on my deathbed, and why I am dictating in Greek.

To the first question I have no single answer. Perhaps it is because I have a perverse nature, perhaps it is because I want to show to the few who will read it the futility of things. The manuscript itself may provide you with some answers. As to my dictating in Greek, you know that my first autobiography was in Latin to please the senators, but now I have only myself to please and like you, I love the Greek language; the harmony of its structure enchants me. I love it written and spoken, and this love remained even after the Athenians mocked and wronged me[17]. How could those sophisticated Athenian asses foresee that the man they derided as a crude Roman provincial would one day hold their destiny in his hands? What a trick fate played on the Athenians, just like a Greek farce, but I made those snobs pay dearly when I became emperor by cancelling their rights and privileges. You yourself, Papinian, know their arrogance and air of superiority towards the Romans whom they still consider barbarians.

This all happened many years ago and I, like most Roman youths, had a veneration for all things Greek, besides it was the fashion to visit Athens. I was hoping to be initiated into the Eleusian mysteries, following the emperors Hadrian, Verus, Marcus and Commodus, and to that end I attended the lectures of the hierophant of Demeter at Eleusis, but for some reason which I cannot recall I didn't go through with the initiation.

I met the same Greek attitude as a legate in Syria. In Antioch they made fun of me and my administration of the east[18], but again I had my revenge, severely punishing them after the defeat of Niger. In Alexandria, another Greek city, I was greeted as a victorious emperor, but they had forgotten, deliberately or not I never knew, to take off the inscription on the city gate, 'Niger is the master of this city.'[19] I was amused, but the trembling city officials were not. I had to stop laughing to calm them down. Castor, my faithful one, gave me a potion to dull the pain so that I can go on.

'Yes Castor, you gave me the message from the empress. I can only receive her at dawn with the others.

'The trouble is, Papinian, that Julia does not believe I am dying or she hides it well if she does. Every time she comes into this room she starts to make small talk as if trying to lighten the atmosphere of doom hanging over me, but her manner and conversation betray no anxiety and I have no intention of hearing her diatribe against the British weather or Caledonian women. How many times have you and I told her we cannot apply our morality laws here when British women have no moral code as we know it?

I beg your indulgence Papinian. I forgot to tell Castor to remove the silver statue of Fortune from my chamber and to place it alternately in the bed chambers of my sons until the duplicate I ordered arrives. I apologise again, Papinian. I did not call you here to talk about the Athenians or Julia. I want to thank you for your guidance during these last seven years. The best thing Julia ever did was to let me recruit from her salon the most celebrated Roman jurist. I have told you so many times already that your presence beside my sons might give the empire a chance of survival. Julia will govern through her sons or without them and perhaps attain the status of her ideal, the Empress Livia who governed through Augustus and Tiberius. The peace I have brought to the empire will not last, for after a time the aggression innate in man will spill over into war. Wise men and prophets have tried to stem this impulse but they could no more stop war than order the waves to stand still in the sea. The devotees of peace have preached that war is a product of man's will and therefore has to be eradicated from their minds. How I pity their illusions! I have been able to give Rome a period of peace in which to build and to create beauty, but in the twilight I know it will not last.

'I must confess, Papinian, that what I really wanted to talk to you about is that unknown state which is death, and if I seem at moments to welcome death it is because I hope that, like a drug, it will release me from physical pain. But what a waste! My mind is alert, the sum of knowledge that I have gained is intact. My body is succumbing but my brain is bursting with unused energy. If I could for a moment have jurisdiction over the beyond, I would decree, and you could frame it in the proper legal terms, that no man should die until his energy is totally spent!

Tell me, Papinian, how is a man supposed to feel when he is dying? I can tell you one thing: don't ever believe a man who tells you he welcomes death, not even me. I have that sinking feeling of embarking on something so alien that I clutch at familiar things – people around me, this room, this bed – and if I sometimes feel that our identity is confined to this life, to leave it for nothing is so painful. And yet, at other times, I feel it is more logical that this unspent energy, this sum of experience, will continue somewhere, somehow. But there is only the void.

'You know how fortune led me to the throne. I have had everything a man could want, but my ambition has given me nothing. *Omnia fui et nihil expedit.* Yes it is best expressed in Latin. I have been everything and I have gained nothing.[20]

One last thing before the crowd arrives. Before I came to Britain I deposited the Egyptian sacred books with the vestal virgins. But it is dangerous to leave them in Rome, for the vestal virgins have been induced by force to give up documents entrusted to them before. I cannot begin to imagine the catastrophes that will occur if these books fall into the hands of ignorant unscrupulous persons, and for this reason my last instruction to you is to take them back to Egypt. Hand them to the chief priest of the Serapeum. He will know what to do with them.

'One last thing, Papinian. I believe that henceforth all emperors should receive the title Antoninus, as they receive that of Augustus.'[21]

The crowd is coming.

'Is that you my dear Julia? Antoninus and Geta, my friends. Don't stand around the bed. I find it difficult to breathe. It has been a long journey and you have all helped me on the way. You see a shrunken and dried body lying before you. The world has called me severe, the man that never laughs, but the joke is on them for I love laughter above all things and I have laughed my head off at the buffoons who have filled my life. Don't make that face, Julia. You had fun with your sophists and I had mine. Come now, don't make such dreary faces. Do not add to the heaviness of the hour.

To be serious again, my friends; I received a state hard pressed on every side. I leave it at peace, even in Britain. I bequeath to my two Antonini an empire which is strong if they are good, feeble if they prove bad. To my sons I say, 'Be harmonious, take care of the army and ignore the rest.' It is time to give the watchword to the tribune on duty. For tonight my friends it shall be *laboremus:* – let us toil.[22]

EPILOGUE

It is totally inappropriate for that just man to be born, or to die

Declaration of the Roman senate on the death of Septimus
Severus

Scriptore Historiae Augustae XVIII.7

After the death of Septimus Severus, Antoninus assumed full control although nominally he shared the throne with his brother. He came to terms with the enemy in Britain and withdrew the troops posted there.[1] He dismissed the praetorian prefect, executed Castor his father's chamberlain, Euodus his old tutor and the doctors who had attended his father. No one who had been honoured by the old emperor or served as his attendant was allowed to survive.[2]

Carrying Septimius' ashes, Julia and her two sons sailed from York to Gaul and from there proceeded by land to Rome. The trouble began during the overland journey: Antoninus wanted to slay his brother but didn't dare because the legions were sympathetic towards Geta who resembled his father in appearance; the brothers did not stay at the same lodgings nor even share a meal.[3]

In Rome the people welcomed them waving branches of laurel and the senate presented an address of greeting. The two emperors wearing the imperial purple headed the funeral procession, followed by the consuls carrying the urn. The consuls saluted the emperors and bowed to the urn which was then deposited in the Antonine mausoleum.[4] A wax effigy of the old emperor was placed on an ivory couch at the entrance to the palace. The figure on the couch was visited for seven days by doctors who examined its deterioration until they pronounced it dead. The ceremony of apotheosis followed.[5] The effigy was lifted from the couch and taken along the sacred way to the old forum where two choirs of patrician children and women of honourable reputation sang hymns in honour of the dead emperor. Next the bier was carried to the Campus Martius and placed on the second storey of a square building looking like a house with four storeys each one smaller than the one below. Prominent citizens sent gifts of perfume and incense, fruits and aromatic herbs. The house was filled with these offerings and a cavalry procession rode in a circle round and round it; chariots too circled the building carrying figures wearing masks of famous generals and emperors. Finally the two emperors lit the torch and put it to the funeral pyre.[6]

After the deification of Septimius Severus, the rivalry between his sons grew. Each felt the other was plotting against him, they backed different factions[7] and conflicted with each other on trials and appointments. The majority of Romans were for Geta, for he was a person of honour and generosity and he surrounded himself with distinguished men of learning, but each was backed by different factions in the city. They even partitioned the palace and bricked up its passages.[8]

It was then suggested that the empire itself should be divided. Antoninus was to have all provinces in Europe and Geta those in Asia while Africa was to be divided between them. The council of their father's advisors assented but Julia cried, 'My sons, you have partitioned the land and the seas but what about your mother? How do you propose to partition her? Very well. Kill me first and each of you take a part of my torn body to your territory and bury it there. In this way I can be shared like the land and the sea.' With these words she began to weep and drew her sons together in an embrace. Everyone was overcome with pity, the scheme was rejected[9], and the council broke up. Antoninus subsequently induced Julia to summon both sons unattended to her apartment for a reconciliation. Centurions, instructed by Antoninus, rushed in and struck at Geta, who ran to his mother and clung to her bosom, pleading, 'Mother, thou didst bear me! Help! I am being murdered.'

Julia was unable to prevent her son's assasination and was not permitted to mourn for her son who was only twenty two years and nine months old. On the contrary, she was compelled to rejoice and laugh! The death of Geta in AD 212 followed only one year after that of his father.

After the murder of Geta, Antoninus had run from the chamber shouting that he had escaped great danger and ordered the palace guards to take him to camp. There he burst into the temple where the standards were worshipped, threw himself on the ground and sacrificed for his safety and removed any doubts from the soldiers' minds with many promises and a gift to each soldier of 2,500 Attic drachmae, ten times more than anything given by Severus. He told them, 'It is because of you I care to live. I pray to live and to die with you.'[10] He increased their normal pay by half and squandered most of what Severus had amassed in eighteen years. The following day he entered the senate, escorted by his guards. He craved the indulgence of the senators, not because he had slain his brother but because he had a sore throat and felt indisposed to address them.[11]

Antoninus' reign as sole emperor commenced with his putting to death all the followers of Geta, even those who had sent him letters or gifts.[12] Cornificia, daughter of Marcus Aurelius and aunt by adoption to Antoninus, was killed because she dared weep for Geta with his mother. When Antoninus asked her to choose the manner of her death she said 'Poor unhappy soul of mine, imprisoned in a vile body, go forth, be freed.' She laid aside the ornaments in which she was arrayed and severed her veins.[13] As to Papinian, Antoninus had him killed because he would not condone the murder of Geta; his body was subjected to all kind of indignities. Aelius Antipater, the *ab epistilis Graecus*, who was a member of the council of Severus and a senator, was forced into retirement, and he committed suicide. Antoninus destroyed Geta's statues and melted down his coins. From the beginning he assiduously heeded his father's advice to take care of the army and despise the rest; he showered the troops with money and privileges. During campaigns however, he was simple and frugal. He marched with the soldiers, ate their food and helped in every task.[14] He became known as Caracalla, a word of Celtic or German origin, from the short cloak, which he adopted. He then made the soldiers wear it and distributed it to the people.

Caracalla spent all his time with the army and left the

civil administration of the empire to Julia.[15] He appointed her to receive petitions and to have charge of his correspondence in Greek and Latin but he did not always heed the excellent advice she gave him.[16] Thus Julia, with her erudition, foresight and intelligence shared at last in the government of the empire, guided, as her husband had been, by the two jurists whom Caracalla spared: Ulpian and Paul. The greatest act of Caracalla's reign, the *Constitutio Antoniniana,* by which he made all the people in the empire Roman citizens went unheeded by the writers of his day except for Dio, who viewed the measure as a means of increasing revenue since, up until this point, non-citizens or aliens had not been liable for all taxes.[17] The new constitution completed the work of Severus, who had given equality to the provinces of the empire. His son went further and, by giving citizenship to all his diverse subjects, he brought greater cohesion to the state. It is ironic that it was left to two provincial Punic emperors to realise the founding claim of the Roman empire to embrace the whole world and the entire human race.[18] If for little else, Caracalla's reign should be remembered for this single brilliant achievement and for the completion of the splendid Antonine Baths, known as the Baths of Caracalla, a building project started by Septimius.

Caracalla had an obsession with Alexander the Great; he once wrote to the senate that Alexander had come to life in the person of himself and that the great conqueror might live on once more in him, having had such a short existence before.[19] This obsession led to his campaign against the Aristotelian philosophers, for Aristotle was supposed to have been involved in Alexander's death.[20] He abolished their common messes in Alexandria and all other privileges.[21] As to Alexander's city, Alexandria, he destroyed the whole population by slaughter and pillage merely on hearing that Alexander was ill-spoken of and ridiculed by them.[22]

The emperor suffered from ill health and disturbing visions, often thinking he was being pursued by his father and brother armed with swords. He invoked spirits against these haunting visions and called upon his father, but they say that Geta haunted him unsummoned. He prayed to the gods, gave votive offerings and sacrifices but was not granted any relief from the afflictions that plagued his body or mind. No help came from Apollo, Asculapius or Serapis.[23] He had premonitions of his own end and in his last letter to the senate he wrote, 'Cease praying that I may be emperor for a hundred years.'[24]

His end came on the 8th day of April AD 216 as he set out with his army from Edessa to Carrhae. He had dismounted from his horse when he was attacked by Martialis, a Moor who was once the steward of Plautianus[25] and who had been commissioned. The tribunes who were party to the plot pretended to come to his rescue but slew him.[26]

Julia was in Antioch when the news came. The new emperor Macrinus treated her with respect but when she started intriguing, he ordered her out of Antioch. The shock of her son's death and reports of subsequent rejoicing in Rome led to her suicide.[27] Caracalla died at twenty nine and four days and his rule lasted for six years and two days.[28] At Nicomedia, some time before his death, Caracalla had quoted Euripedes to the Senator Dio, who noted the verses in his history.

And the things we looked for, the gods deign not to fulfil them
And the paths undiscerned of our eyes, the gods unseal them.[29]

Thus the prediction of the oracle of Zeus Belus of Apamea given to Severus was fulfilled. 'Thy house shall perish in blood.'

A *note on the memoir*

Septimius Severus wrote an autobiography, but it was lost. This secret memoir is neither a historical novel nor a work of fiction. It is a biography based on the known facts about his life and reign, reconstructed from ancient sources, mainly Dio Cassius who knew the emperor personally, and Herodian who wrote only thirty three years after his death. The Augustan History, which was written much later is less reliable. Besides the ancient sources, many works of modern scholarship which utilise the evidence of inscriptions, numismatics and monuments have been consulted.

The liberty taken in this memoir has been in the selection of certain events and the emphasis placed upon them; other events have been stretched beyond the known facts. We know, for example, Severus' interest in astrology and divination and we know that he collected the books of prophecy and magic from all the sanctuaries in Egypt, but no source tells us what he made of them or to what use he put them. We also know that he closed the tomb of Alexander, but we do not know how the Alexandrians reacted to this event. There are no invented characters except for the priest and priestess of Isis and the Bedouin guide, Aziz. To the unknown woman with whom Severus was accused of adultery a name (Drusilla) was given.

The scenes at his first wedding and the Punic funeral were inspired by rituals practised up until the middle of the twentieth century in a village in Palestine called Ramallah. Ramallah is no longer a village and the ancient customs have disappeared. What we do know is that the Phoenicians, the descendants of the Canaanites of Palestine and the Levant, carried with them from Tyre and Sidon to Africa not only their ancestral language, but also their religion and their customs. Some archaic practices have a tenacity and a longevity that can span the centuries; perhaps some of these survived in Leptis.

On studying the reign of Severus, the feeling grows that he has not been given his rightful place in history. Ancient writers accuse him of undermining the discipline of the army and of opening the empire to barbarians. Some modern writers attribute the decline of the empire to his rule. In reality he unified the empire, increased the tempo of Romanisation, added extensive territory and presided over a long period of peace and security. His age was the golden age of Roman jurisprudence. Many dwell on his cruelty, but few Roman emperors escape this charge. To his credit are sympathy for the oppressed, humane laws and the struggle for equality within the empire culminating in the 'Constitutio Antoniniana' promulgated by his son.

Severus is fascinating because in himself and in his career he proved the universality of the Roman empire. A Phoenician from Africa, married to a Syrian, he was quaestor in Spain, legate in Pannonia, governor of Lyon and emperor in Rome. He died on campaign in York and, in spite of the prejudice against his origin, he succeeded in holding together and personifying the *Orbis Romanus*.

Chronology

146	S. Severus born at Leptis Magna.
	Study of law, Greek and Latin in Rome
No precise	First post as pleader for the treasury, and
dates	quaestor in Spain and Sardina.
†173	Tribune of the plebs in Leptis under his great uncle and namesake, S. Severus, pro-Consul of Africa.
175	Married Paccia Marciana.
‡182-184	Commander of Legion IV Scythica in Syria.
*185	Visit to Athens.
186-188	Legate of Gallia Lugdunenis (Lyon).
187	Paccia Marciana dies childless.
	Marriage to Julia Domna, Princess of Emesa.
188	Birth of first son, Bassianus Antoninus (Caracalla).
188-189	Legate of Sicilly.
189	Birth of second son, Geta.
	Legate of Upper Pannonia.
	Acclaimed Emperor by the army after the murder of the Emperor Pertinax.
	Niger Legate of Syria, proclaimed Emperor by the troops.
	S. Severus enters Rome.
	The Emperor Julianus, who ruled for 70 days, killed by soldiers.
	S. Severus names Albinus, Legate of Britain, Caesar.

†	Some sources give the date as 167-169.
‡	Some sources give the date as 180.
*	Some sources give the date as 182.

166

193-194	Civil war with Niger. Niger defeated at Perinthus, Cyzicus and Nicaea, and killed near Antioch.
193-196	Seige of Byzantium, its fall and destruction by the troops of S. Severus.
194	First Parthian Campaign.
195	Self-adoption of S. Severus by House of Antonine.
196	Caracalla named Caesar.
197	Albinus declared Augustus in Britain, and defeated by S. Severus in Lyon.
197-198	Second Parthian Campaign and sack of Ctesiphon.
198-199	First and second attempt at conquering Hatra.
199	Caracalla named Augustus.
199-200	S. Severus in Egypt.
202	Return to Rome. Edict against conversion to Christianity and Judaism.
202 *cont.*	Decennalia Marriage of Caracalla.
203	Builds Septizodium. Dedication of the Arch of Triumph, offered by the Senate and the people of Rome. African visit.
204	Saecular games Arch of the Argentarii.
205	Plautianus killed. Aemilius Papinianus (Papinian) replaces him as Praetorian Prefect.
208	Depart for Britain.
209	Geta raised to Augustus. S. Severus received the title of Britannicus Maximus.
211	Death of S. Severus at York, February 4th.

ABBREVIATIONS

Fontaine, J., *La Littérature Latine*	Lit.Lat.
Victor, A., de Caesaribis	de Caes.
Dio Cassius	Dio.
Scriptores Historia Augustae	HA
Barnes, T.D., "The Family..."	Hist. 16. 1967
Gage, J., "L'empereur romain devant	Ktéma No.1
Sérapis".	
Guey, J., "L'Inscription du grand père de	*L'Inscription*
Septime-Sévère à Leptis Magna."	
Hatra, "Ville de dieu soleific..."	RI No. 12 Bagdad
Kennedy, D.L., "The Frontier Policy..."	RF St. No. 71
The Cambridge Ancient History	Camb. Ant. Hist.
Swan Hellenic Cruise Handbook	S.H. Hand
Corbier, M., "Les familles clarissimes..."	Epigrapha

Notes

First Night - The Dream

1. Pius: the name of his adopted father, assumed in AD 195;
   Pertinax: the name of the murdered emperor assumed in
   AD 193; Arabicus and Adiabenicus: the titled given by
   the senate after the First Pathian War in AD 195;
   Parthicus Maximus: decreed by the senate after the
   Second Parthian War in AD 198; Father of the Country:
   given by the senate in AD 194; Britannicus Maximus:
   assumed during the British Campaign of AD 210;
   Invincible (Invictissimi Augustus) appeared on coins
   after the Parthian Wars; Defender of the world
   (conservatori orbi).
2. Dio., 75.73; HA III, 1.2; de Caes., p.23.
3. M. Aurelius, 1.5.
4. Livy, intro by B. Radice, p.5.
5. Herodian III, 1.48.

6.   Ibid. 14.7.8.
7.   The fortress of VI Victrix, used as a residence by governors; de Caes, p.110 (footnote).
8.   Apokrimata, p.47.
9.   M. Aurelius, II, 14.
10. de Caes., p.23.
11. Herodian III, 14.9.
12. A. Birley, p.173.
13   Dio., 76.2.3.
14. Quoted by A. Birley, p.186.
15. Herodian III, 14.1.15.
16. Dio., 77.14.1.
17. Ibid. 76.14.1.7.
18. A. Birley, p.182.
19. Ibid. p.175; Dio. 77.7.4-5.
20. HA XVII, 1.3.
21. Herodian III, 14.15.
22. The dream is based on an actual event; Dio., 77.7.4-5.
23. Dio., 77.73.
24. Servanius and his grandson were killed on the orders of his brother-in-law, the Emperor Hadrian.
25. Secret police.
26. Herodian III, 14.15.
27. Herodian II, 15.1-3.
28. Herodian II, 15.3-5.
29. Dio., 74.17.1-2.
30. Ibid.
31. Dio., 74.15.2.
32. Herodian II, 14.1-2.
33. Herodian II ,14.3; Dio. 75.2.2.
34. Dio. 75.2.1.
35. Ibid.75.2.5-6.
36. Ibid.
37. Corcopino, p.7.
38. Dio. 76.9.3-5; E. Gibbons, Vol I, p.107.
38. HA XV, 5.
40. Dio., 77.11.12.
41   R. Turcan, p.153.
42. Dio., 79.8.6-8.
43. The oracle revealed the prophecy, but only after the

death of Severus and the murder of his son. D. Potter p.170.

44. Dio., 75.7.3.
45. F. Zoss & G. Zing, p.67.
46. Dio., 74. 11.1-6.
47. Dio., 74.11.7.
48. HA VI, 7.1.
49. M. Corbier, pp.19, 93.
50. Dio., 76.7.3-8.
51. G. Charles-Picard, *August et Neron*, Intro.
52. Dio., 76.9.4.
53. HA XII, 9.
54. Dio., 7.4.
55. Dio., 74.15.6/16.1.
56. Dio., 76.8.1-3.
57. Herodian III, 5.1-2.
58. Dio., 76.8.4.
59. A. Birley, p.121.
60. Herodian III, 6.1-6.
61. de Caes., p22.
62. Dio., 76. 7.1-2; M. Hadas p.119.
63. Digest XIV, 1.4.
64. A. Piganiol, p.400.

Second Night - Punica Fides

1. G. Charles-Picard, *August et Neron*, pp.5-9.
2. Livy, intro. by B. Radice. p.9.
3. Quoted by T.W.H. Libeschuetz, p.147.
4. Quoted by A. Birley, p.19.
5. Silvae, 4.5.
6. Juvenal, *Satire 10*, quoted B. Radice, Int. p.8.
7. Livy, quoted B Radice, Int, pp.7-8.
8. Livy, p.52.
9. HA XIX, 9.10 "Afrum quiddam usque ad senectutem sonnas".
10. HA XV, 6.7.
11. Dio., 77.16.1-3.
12. Juvenal op. cit. p.7.
13. Dio., 18.65.7; J. Babelon, p.66; A. Birley, p.142.

14. J. Babelon, p.60.
15. M. Aurelius, II.2.
16. J Guey, *L'Inscription* pp.186, 198.
17. de Caes. pp.110,111; M. Hammond, p.140.
18. G. Charles-Picard, *Les Religions*, pp.35, 39.
19. Herodotus VII, p.499.
20. Herodotus VII, p.500.
21. G. Charles-Picard, *Les Religions*, p.37.
22. Ibid. p.10.
23. Ibid. pp.40,44,45.
24. Herodotus IV, p.319.
25. Herodotus op. cit. pp.283, 399, 425.
26. Herodotus op. cit. p.311.
27. St Augustine, Epistolae ad Romanos ichoata exposito, quoted D. Harden, pp. 20,105. According to St. Agustine, rustics in Africa called themselves "Chanani" in the early 5th century AD. It is therefore safe to assume that they called themselves "Chanani" in the 2nd century AD.
28. D. Harden, p.19.
29. D. Harden, p.30.
30. A. Mazar, p.355.
31. D. Harden, p.68.
32. G. Ch. Picard, *Les Religions*, p.103.
33. J. Guey, *L'Inscription*, p 188.
34. J. D. Barnes, *Hist. 16* (1967), pp. 105, 159.
35. Ibid.
36. J. Guey, *L'Inscription*, p 188.
37. De. Caes., p.51 (footnote 28).
38. HA III, 4.5.
39. M. Hammond, p.153.
40. HA I, 6.7; A. Piganiol, p.396.
41. A. Birley, p.46.
42. HA IV, 3.4.
43. A. Birley, p.62; M. Grant, p.325.
44. HA II, 6.9; M. Hammond, p.155.
45. HA II, 1.2.
46. Dio., 73.14.3; Dio., 77.16.3; Herodian II, 9.2.
47. Quoted J. Corcopino, p.68.
48. Juvenal, *Satire 3*, quoted R. Turqan, p.131.

49.   C.R. Whittaker, p.78.

Third Night - Julia

1.   J. Guey, *L'Inscription*, pp214, 216.
2.   R. Turcan, p.178.
3.   HA III, 9.5.
4.   Herodian III, 13.1.2.
5.   J. Corcopino, pp.84-85.
6.   Ibid.
7.   HA XIX, 7.10.
8.   Dio., 77.17.1-4.
9.   HA XVIII, 4.7.
10.   Dio., 77.17.1-4.
11.   HA XIX, 7.10.
12.   R. Turcan, p.175.
13.   A. Birley, p.71.
14.   S. Perowne, p.147.
15.   J. Babelon, p.45.
16.   R. Turcan, p.175.
17.   Philostratus, *Life of Apolollonius*.
18.   *Lit.Lat.*, p.163.
19.   T.W.H. Libeschuitz, pp.222, 223.
20.   P. Grimal, p.164; J. Babelon, p.45; Camb. Ant. Hist., p.18.
21.   F. Zoss & G. Zing, p.72.
22.   A.M. McCann, pp.109, 110, 206.
23.   R. Turcan, p.145.
24.   A. Birley, p.71.
25.   R. Turcan, p.167.
26.   Ibid. p.182.
27.   Ibid. pp.181, 183.
28.   G.W. Bowerstock p.117.
29.   Ibid. p.113.
30.   Ibid.
31.   G.W. Bowerstock, pp.14, 116.
32.   Ibid. pp.113, 124, 134.
33.   Ibid. p.119, 120.
34.   Ibid. p.121.
35.   J. Babelon, p.32.
36.   Dio., 79.25.1.

37. Dio., 76.15.5-7.
38. Dio., 76.15.6a, 7.5.
39. Dio. 76. 15.6.
40. HA IX, 11.
41. Dio., 76.15.6.
42. R. Turcan, p.175.
43. Herodian III, 13.1.1-2 (footnote 2).
44. Dio., 76.15.6; 78.24.1.
45. HA XVIII, 9.
46. The first bronze coins bearing the legend "son of the deified Marcus Pius" were issued in AD 195. A.M. McCann, p.193.
47. Dio., 75.14.6-15.
48. Dio., 76.15.1-2.
49. Dio., 76.15.6.
50. Dio., 76.14.4-6.
51. Dio., 76.15.7.

Fourth Night - The Talking Towers of Byzantium.

1. Dio., 75.7.3; A. Birley p.203 (appendix).
2. Dio., 75.14.4-6.
3. Herodian III, 1.5.7.
4. Dio., 79.3.9.
5. Herodian VI, 1.5-7.
6. Dio., 75.10.3-6.
7. Dio., 75.11.1-3.
8. Dio., 75. 12.4-6.
9. Ibid.
10. Dio., 75.13.4-6.
11. Ibid.
12. Herodian III, 6.6-9; Dio., 75.14.1-2.
13. Dio., 75.14.2-12.
14. J.B. Bury, pp.68-9, 75.
15. Herodian III, 2.7-9.
16. Ibid. 2.9; 3.1.
17. Ibid. 2.7-9; 3.2-4.
18. Ibid. 3.5-6.
19. Dio., 75. 7.5-8; Herodian III, 3.7.
20. Herodian III, 4.2-3.

21. Ibid. 4.1-2.
22. Dio., 75.6.1-3.
23. Dio., 75.6.3-4.
24. A. Birley, p.113.
25. Dio., 75.6.3.
26. Herodian III, 2.6.
27. Ibid. 2.4-6.
28. Dio., 75.6.1-2a.
29. Herodian III, 2.3-4.
30. HA VIII, 15.1.6.
31. HA VIII, 8.11-17.
32. Herodian III, 2.3-4.
33. R. Brilliant, p.174 (footnote 2).
34. HA XV, 1.5; Dio. 76.9.1-2.
35. A. Birley, p.115.
36. de Caes., p.23.
37. A. Birley, p.16.
38. Dio., 76.9.2-5.
39. HA XVI, 3.4.
40. HA XVII, 1.3.
41. Dio., 75.3.3.
42. Th. Mommsen. p.625.
43. Herodian III, 9.2-4.
44. RI No.12 Bagdad, p.25.
45. Ibid. p.23.
46. Dio., 75.2.1-3.
47. Dio., 76.10.1-3; Herodian VI, 9.2-4, 7-8.
48. Dio., 75.11.1-3.
49. Herodian III, 9.2-4; Dio., 76.11.3-4.
50. Dio., 76.10.2-3.
51. Ibid.
52. Dio., 76.12.1-3.
53. Ibid.
54. HA XV, 6.7; Dio., 76.10.2-3.
55. HA XV, 12.1-9.
56. Ibid.
57. Dio., 76.11.1-2.
58. Dio., 76. 13.1-2.
59. A. Piganiol, p.396.
60. Herodian III, 8.4.

61. M. Grant, p.258; M. Hammond, p.170.
62. Herodian III, 8.4-5.
63. Dio., 75.2.5-6.
64. M. Grant, p.257; M. Hammond, p.170; P. Grimal, p.157.
65. Herodian III, 8.4.
66. Camb. Ant. Hist. p.16; M. Hammond, p.171.
67. M. Grant, p.258.
68. P. Grimal, p.157; A. Piganiol, p.401; A. Birley, p.196.
69. M. Grant, p.259.
70. Dio., 77.15.2.

Fifth Night - Egyptian Music

1. HA XVII, 3.7.
2. RF Studies Int. No.71, p.879.
3. HA XVII, 1.4; P. Grimal, p. 164; Zoss and Zing, p.7; A. Piganiol, p.403.
4. A. Birley, p.136.
5. S. Raven, p.147.
6. Dio., 76.13.2-3.
7. HA XII, 1.3.
8. S. Raven, p.147.
9. A. Birley, p.139.
10. A.M. McCann, p.110
11. A. Birley, p.138.
12. A.M. McCann, p.111.
13. Ibid. p.109 (footnote).
14. Ibid.
15. Camb. Ant. Hist., p.18.
16. Dio., 77.16.1-2.
17. HA XII, 3.7; A. Birley, p.139.
18. J. Gage, Ktéma, No.1, p.157.
19. A.M. McCann, p.110.
20. A. Birely, p.138.
21. HA XVII, 1.4.
22. S. Raven, p.145.
23. Apokrimata, p.27; HA XVII, 1.2; Dio., 76.1.7.1.
24. Sertonius, p.58.
25. Arrian, Anabasis II, 15.27, III.6.1, appendix IV, p.466.
26. Herodotus, p.147.

27. Arrian, *Anabasis* I. 35, II.3.1.
28. Dio., 76.13.2.3; S. Raven, pp.44,45; A. Birley, p.136.
29. In spite of constant search by archaeologists and tomb robbers, the site was never found.
30. This description is taken from the papyrus of Ani as illustrated by E.A.W. Budge, *The Book of the Dead.*
31. Dio., 76.13.2-3.
32. Ibid.
33. Ibid.
34. E.A.W. Budge, *Egpytian Magic*, p.16.
35. Ibid. p.42.
36. Ibid. p.134.
37. A. Birley, p.136.
38. E.A.W. Budge, *Egpytian Magic*, p.12.
39. Ibid. p.197.
40. Ibid. p.195.
41. Ibid. pp 104.105.
42. HA IV, 1-2.
43. Digest XIVII, 4.5.
44. E.A.W. Budge, *The Book of the Dead*, p.59.
45. Ibid. p.347.
46. Ibid.
47. E.A.W. Budge *Egptian Magic*, p.71.
48. E.A.W. Budge, *The Book of the Dead*, p.659.
49. E.A.W. Budge, *Egyptian Magic*, p.10.
50. Ulpian, Digest XXVII, 9.
51. Just. Digest, 1.2.2.
52. Just. Digest XIVII, 11.4.

Sixth Night - Felicitus Temporum

1. Herodian III, 10.2-3.
2. Dio., 77.1.1-5.
3. Ibid.
4. Herodian III, 8.8-9.
5. J. Guey, *L'Inscription*, p.213.
6. HA XIV, 2.7.
7. Herodian VI, 10.6-8.
8. Herodian III, 10.5-6.
9. Dio., 77.1.2-4.

10. G. Charles-Picard, *Les Religions*, p.196.
11. Herodian III, 10.8-10.
12. Ibid.
13. R. Brilliant, p.95 (footnote 38).
14. R.A.G. Carson, *Coins*, p.158.
15. Dio., 77.6.3.
16. Dio., 75.3.3; Herodian II, 9.5-7; R. Brilliant, p.100.
17. R. Brilliant, preface and intro.
18. Ibid. p.204.
19. Ibid. p.176.
20. A. Birley, p.156.
21. R. Brilliant, pp.107,120.
22. Ibid., pp.119, 120.
23. Ibid., pp 120, 125 (fig.37).
24. P. Grimal, p.155.
25. Dio., 77.16.3.
26. R. Brilliant, p.113.
27. Herodian III, 8.12.
28. R. Brilliant, in his introduction to Chapter III gives the colours as a possibility, but no trace remains.
29. R. Brilliant, pp.113,120.
30. Ibid, p.30.
31. S. Perowne, p.155.
32. A. Birley, p.164; P. Grimal, p.158.
33. HA XXIII, 1.3.
34. S. Perowne, p.159.
35. HA XXIII, 1.3.
36. A. Birley, p.163.
37. R. Graves, p.344.
38. Herodian III, 8.9 (footnote 1).
39. A.M. McCann, p.110.
40. Herodian III, 8.9. (footnote 1)
41. Herodian III, 8.9-10.
42. A. Birley, pp.156-8.
43. Herodian III, 8.9-10 (footnote 1).
44. A. Birley, p.158.
45. Dio., 76. 4.5.
46. Herodian III, 10.6-7.
47. Dio., 76. 14.6.
48. Herodian III, 10.6-11 (footnote 2).

49. Dio., 76, 15.1-2.
50. Ibid. 15.20.
51. Dio., 77.2.25.
52. Dio., 76.15.1-2.
53. Ibid. 15.7.
54. Ibid. 14.3-4.
55. Ibid.
56. Ibid. 15.2b.
57. Ibid. 15.2.
58. Ibid. 14.2.
59. Ibid. 14.7.
60. Ibid. 17.2.1-2.
61. Ibid. 2.3-4.
62. Ibid. 14.4-6.
63. Herodian III, 10.6 (footnote 4).
64. Ibid. 10.6-8.
65. A. Birley, p.154.
66. Dio., 77.2.25.
67. Ibid. 2.4-5.
68. Herodian III, 10.6 (footnote 4).
69. Ibid. 10.8. (footnote 4).
70. Ibid. 11.2-3.
71. Ibid. 10.6.
72. Dio. 76.15.2-3.
73. Ibid. 16.2-3.
74. HA XIV, 7.8-10.
75. Dio. 77, 3.1-2.
76. Ibid. 3-4.
77. Herodian III, 11.4-5.
78. Ibid. 11.9-10.
79. Apokrimata, p.11; Dio. 76, 7.7.
80. Dio., 75.4.1-5.
81. Dio., 77.4.4-5.
82. Ibid. 5.4-6.
83. Ibid. 5.1-3.
84. Herodian III, 13.1-2.
85. A. Piganiol, p.402.
86. Dio., 73.13.14.15.16-17.
87. Camb. Ant. Hist. pp.31,32.
88. Ibid. p.33.

89.   Just., *Digest* XIVII.11.4.
90.   Ibid.
91.   Just., *Digest* XXX.11.
92.   Camb. Ant. Hist. pp.24,25.
93.   A. Piganiol, p.402.
94.   A. Birley, p.165.

Seventh Night - Omnia Fui et Nihil Expedit

1.   Dio., 77.19.6-7 (on Roman imperial funerals in general).
2.   Herodian III, 15.7-8 says the urn was made of
      alabastar, Dio., 77.15.4 says it was porphyry,
      HA XXIV.2 says it was made of gold.
3.   Dio., 75.1.1-2; E. Gibbon, p.100.; A Birley, p.103.
4.   Dio., 75.1.2-5.
5.   HA III, 3.1; Herodian II, 9.4; Dio., 75.7.3.
6.   Dio., 76.13.1-2.
7.   HA IV, 1.2.
8.   J. Guey, *L'Inscription*, p.167.
9.   Ibid. p.174.
10.   Ibid. p.167.
11.   HA XVII,1.3; Dio., 75.9.4.
12.   J. Babelon, p.52.
13.   Dio., 77.16.1-3.
14.   Ibid.
15.   M.Wheeler, S.H. Hand, pp.360.362.
16.   HA XXIII, 1.3.
17.   HA III, 4.7
18.   HA III,6.7, 19.7-8.
19.   A. Birley, p.137.
20.   HA XVIII, 11.
21.   Ibid. 7.3-6.
22.   Ibid. 1.3.

Epilogue

1.   Dio., 78.1.1.
2.   Herodian III, 15.4-5.
3.   Herodian IV, 1.1-3.
4.   Herodian III, 15.7-8.

5.   Herodian IV, 1.2-1.
6.   Herodian IV, 2.1-10.
7.   Dio., 77.2.2.; C.R. Whittaker, p.361.
8.   Herodian IV, 3.6-9.
9.   Ibid. 3.6-9.
10. Herodian IV, 6.7 (footnote 2).
11. Dio., 78.4.1a (footnote 1).
12. Ibid. 12.5-6.
13. Dio., 77.11.6a.
14. Dio., 78.1.11-12.
15. Ibid. 4.2-3; Dio., 77.18.2.
16. Dio., 78.18.2-5.
17. Ibid. 7.5.
18. J.B. Bury, Vol. I, p.124.
19. Dio., 78.7.2-4.
20. Arrian, *Anabasis III*, 2.7.
21. Dio., 78.7.2-3.
22. Ibid. 23.2.
23. Ibid. 15.3-7.
24. Dio., 79.8.3.
25. Ibid. 11.2-3.
26. Ibid. 5.1-6.
27. A. Birley, p.192.
28. Dio., 78.6.5.
29. Dio., 79.8.4.

Selected Bibliography

PRINCIPAL SOURCES

Appian, *History*, tr. Horace White. Loeb Library, London, 1912-13.

Apokrimata, *Decisions of Septimius Severus on Legal Matters*, trans. W. Linn Westermann. Legal commentary by A. Arthur Schiller, Columbia University Press, New York, 1954.

Aurelius Victor, *de Caesaribus*, trans. H. W. Bird, Liverpool University Press; *Epitome de Caesaribus*, ed. Franciscus Pichlmayr, trans. J.E. Bernard, Teubner, 1911, Leipzig.

Carson, R.A.C., *Coins of Greece and Rome* (2nd revised edition), London.

Corpus Inscriptionum Graecarum
Corpus Inscriptionum Latinarum
The Digest of Justinian, ed. Mommsen, trans. P. Kreguer and A. Watson, Philadeliphia, 1985, Vol. I.

Dio Cassius, *Roman History*, trans. Earnest Cary, Vols. 73-79 19591, on the basis of the version of H.B. Foster, London, William Heinemann, London, 1914.

Herodian, *History*, Vols. II, III, IV, trans. C.R. Whittaker, Harvard University Press, London, 1969.

Scriptores Historiae Augustae, trans. David Magie, Harvard University Press, London; I: 1921; II: 1924; III:1932 (III Vols).

Syllage Numorum Graecorum, Vol. IV, Part VIII, Fitzwilliam Museum, Oxford, 1970.

GENERAL SOURCES

Aurelius, Marcus, *The Meditations*, Harvard Classics, Vol.2, New York,. 1909.

Babelon, J., *Le portrait dans l'antiquité d'après les monnaies*, Paris, 150; *Impératrices syriennes*, Paris, 1957.

Barnes, T.D., "The family and career of Septimius Severus", *Historia 16*, 1067, 87-107.

Benario, H.W., "Rome of the Severi", Coll. *Latomus* 17, 1958, 712-22

Besnier, M., *L'empire romain de l'avènement des Sévères au Concile de Nicée*, Paris, 1937.

Bianchi Bandinelli, R., *Rome, le centre due pouvoir*, Paris, 1970.

Birley, A., *Septimius Severus, The African Emperor*, London, 1971;
Lives of the Later Caesars, Penguin, 1976.

Bloch, R., and Cousin, J., *Rome et son destin*, Paris, 1954.

Bowersock, G.W., *Roman Arabia*, Cambridge, Mass., 1983.

Brilliant, R., *The Arch of Septimius Severus in the Roman Forum*, Rome, 1967.

Budge, E.A.W, *The Book of the Dead*, New York, 1960; *The Gods of the Egyptians*, New York, 1969; *Egyptian Magic*, London, 1972.

Bury, J.B., *History of the Latter Roman Empire*, Vol. I, Dover Publications, New York, 1958.

Cagnat, R., *Cours d'épigraphie latine*, 4ᵉ ed. Paris, 1914; *Inscriptiones craecae ad res Romanas Pertinentes*, Paris, 1911-1927.

Carcopino, J., *Daily Life in Ancient Rome*, Paris, 1941.

Ceuleneer, A. de, *Essaii sur la vie et le règne de Septime Sévère*, *Mémoires de l'Académie royale de Belgique*, 1880, XCIII.

Charles-Picard, G., *Les religions de l'Afrique antique*, Paris, 1954, "Le mysticisme africain".; *Comptes rendue de l'Académie des Inscriptions et Belles-Lettres*, Paris, 1946, 443-466; *August et Neron*, Paris, 1954.

The Cambridge Ancient History, ed. Cook, Alcock and Charleswalt, Vol. XII, Cambridge, 1939.

Columba, G.M., *Settimio Severo e gli imperatori africani*, African Romana, Milan, 1935.

Corbier, M., "Les familles clarissimes d'Afrique proconsulaire (Ier-IIIe siècle)", *Epigrafia e ordine senatorio (Tituli 5)*, Rome, 1982, 685-754.

Cumont, F., *Les religions orientales dans le paganisme romain*, Paris, 1919.

Darembert, S., *Dictionnaire des Antiquités grecques et romaines*, Paris, 1978-1916.

Dessau, H., *Prosopographia Imperii romani, III, p.198.*

Downey, G., *A History of Antioch in Syria*, Princeton University Press, 1961; *Ecole française de Rome, mélanges, les jeux séculaires de 304 AD et la dynastie des Sévères.*

Drummond, S., and Nelson, L., *The Western Frontiers of Imperial Rome*, New York, 1994.

Durry, M., *Les cohortes prétoriennes*, Paris, 1938.

Fontaine, F., *Douze autres Césars*, Paris, 1985;
Vignt Césars et trois Parques, Paris, 1994.

Frontaine, J., *La littérature latine chrétienne*, P.U.F., Paris, 1970.

Gage, J., "L'empereur romain devant Sérapis", *Ktéma, No. 1*, 1976, 157-166.

Gibbon, E., *The Decline and Fall of the Roman Empire*,The Modern Library, Vol. I, New York, 1934.

Grant, M., *Roman History from Coins*, Cambridge University Press, 1958.

Graves, R., *Claudius the God*, Penguin edition, 1954.

Grimal, P., *L'empire romain*, Paris, 1993.

Guey, J., "L'inscription du grand-père de Septime-Sévère à Leptis Magna", *Mémoires.. société nationale...antiq...de France* Vol. II, 82, 1951, pp 161-226.

Hacquard, G., *La civilisation romaine*,Paris, 1968;
Guide romain antique, Hachette, Paris, 1952.

Hadas, M., *A History of Rome*, London, 1958.

Hamilton, E., *The Roman Way*, New York, 1965.

Hatra, ville du dieu soleil, Revue illustrée par le Ministère d'Information, No.12, Bagdad, 1970.

Hammond, M., "Septimius Severus, Roman bureaucrat", *Harvard Studies Class Philology 51*, 1940,137-173.

Hannestad, K., "Septimius Severus in Egypt. A contribution to the chronology of the years 198-222", *Classica et Medievalia*, Copenhagen 1944, 194-222.

Harden, D., *The Phoenicians*, London, 1962.

Hardie, A., *Statius and the Silvae*, Liverpool, 1983.

Herodotus, *The Histories*, trans. A. De Selincourt, Penguin, 1974.

Jones, A.H.M., *The Cities of the Eastern Roman Provinces*, Oxford, 1971.

Jones, C.P., "A Syrian in Lyon", *AJP 99*, 1978, pp.336-53.

Kaser, K., *Das römische Privatrecht*, Munich, 1955.

Kotula, T., "Septime Sévère a-t-il visité l'Afrique en tant qu'empereur?" *Eos 73*, 1985, pp.151-65.

Kennedy, D.L., "The Frontier Policy of Septimius Severus - New Evidence from Arabia", pp. 879-88 in W.S. Hanson and L.J.F. Keppie (*eds*) *Roman Frontiers Studies, 1979*. BAR International Series 71, Oxford 1980.

"Les jeux séculaires de 204 AD, et la dynastie des Sévères", *Mélange de l'Ecole française de Rome*, 1934.

Liebeschuetz, T.W.H., *Continuity and Change in Roman Religion*, Oxford, 1979.

Livy, *The War with Hannibal*, trans. A. de Selincourt (Books XXI-XXX) Penguin, 1974.

Maspero, G., *Life in Ancient Egypt and Assyria*, New York, 1892.

Mazar, A., *Archaeology of the Land of the Bible*, New York, 1990.

McCann, A.M., "The Portraits of Septimius Severus AD 193-211, *Memoirs American Academy Rome 30*, 1968.

Millar, F., "Local cultures in the Roman Empire: Libyan, Punic and Latin in Roman Africa", *Journal of Roman Studies, 58*, 126-34, 1968.

Mommsen, Th., *Histoire romaine*, trans. into French by C A Alexandre, Paris, 1985.

Murphy, J.G., *The Reign of the Emperor L. Septimius Severus from the Evidence of the Inscriptions*, Philadelphia, 1945.

Petrowne, S., *The Caesar's Wives Above Suspicion?*, London, 1974.

Piganiol, A. *Histoire de Rome*, Paris, 1939.

Platnauer, M., *The Life and Reign of the Emperor L. Septimius Severus*, Oxford, 1918.

Potter, D., *Prophets and Emperors*, London, 1994.

Raven, S., *Rome in Africa*, London, 1984.

Reville, J., *La religion à Rome sous les Sévères*, Paris, 1886.

Turcan, R., *Les cultes orientaux dans le monde romain*, Paris, 1986.

Safar, F.M., *Hatra* (in Arabic), Baghdad, 1974.

Salama, P, "Nouveaux témoignage de l'oeuvre de Sévères dans la Mauritanie césarienne", *Libya I* (avril-octobre), 1953, 231 et. seq.

Stierlin, H., *Les cités du désert*, Paris, 1978.

Suetonius, *The Twelve Caear s*, trans. R. Graves, 1958.

Swan Hellenic Cruise Handbook, London, 1985.

Syme, R., *The Roman Revolution*, Oxford, 1960.

Statius, *The Silvae*.

Turton, G., *The Syrian Princesses*, London, 1974.

Whittaker, C.R., "The Western Phoenicians: colonisation and assimilation", *Proc. Cambridge Philol. Soc., n.s. 20*, 1974, 58-79.

Zoss, F., and Zing, C., *Les empereurs romains, 27 av J.C.-476 ap. J.C.*, Geneva, 1994.